William Clark Russell

My Shipmate Louise

Vol. 3

William Clark Russell

My Shipmate Louise
Vol. 3

ISBN/EAN: 9783337347048

Printed in Europe, USA, Canada, Australia, Japan

Cover: Foto ©Andreas Hilbeck / pixelio.de

More available books at **www.hansebooks.com**

MY SHIPMATE LOUISE

The Romance of a Wreck

BY

W. CLARK RUSSELL

IN THREE VOLUMES

VOL. III.

London
CHATTO & WINDUS, PICCADILLY
1890

PRINTED BY
SPOTTISWOODE AND CO., NEW-STREET SQUARE
LONDON

CONTENTS

OF

THE THIRD VOLUME

CHAPTER		PAGE
XXIX.	THE CAPTAIN BEGINS A STORY	1
XXX.	THE CAPTAIN MAKES A PROPOSAL	21
XXXI.	THE FORM OF AGREEMENT	45
XXXII.	A TRAGEDY	67
XXXIII.	THE CARPENTER CALLS A COUNCIL	90
XXXIV.	I ASSENT	116
XXXV.	MY CAPTAINCY	140
XXXVI.	I CONVERSE WITH WETHERLY	164
XXXVII.	CAPE HORN	184
XXXVIII.	LAND!	208
XXXIX.	THE ISLAND	233
XL.	I ESCAPE	256
XLI.	WE SAIL AWAY	278
XLII.	CONCLUSION	302

MY SHIPMATE LOUISE

CHAPTER XXIX

THE CAPTAIN BEGINS A STORY

For a couple of days nothing that need find a place in this narrative happened. On the afternoon of the third day of our being aboard the barque we sighted a sail, hull down, to windward. I climbed into the main-top and examined her through the glass, and found her a brig, very loftily rigged, her canvas soaring into moonsails, a sight I had never before witnessed at sea, even in those days when ships went more heavily draped than they do in these. She was heading our course, perhaps making a slightly more weatherly navigation, and full blown as she looked to be—a large, soft cloud of canvas in the lenses of the telescope—we passed her at the rate of two feet to her one; and some time before sunset we had sunk her to her royals on the quarter.

Miss Temple wanted me to ask Captain Braine to run the *Lady Blanche* into speaking distance of the brig, that we might ascertain where she was bound to and get on board of her. 'For she may be sailing,' she said, 'to some South American port that will be, comparatively speaking, close at hand, where we shall be easily able to find a ship to convey us home.' But after thinking a little, I decided to keep quiet. It would not sound very graciously to request Captain Braine to tranship us into an outward-bound vessel: nor would it be wise to put him to the trouble of deviating from his course merely, perhaps, to ascertain that the brig was bound round the Horn to parts more distant than the Mauritius. Besides, I had no wish to court a blunt refusal from Captain Braine to put his vessel within hailing distance of another until a real opportunity to get to England should present itself by some homeward-bound ship passing close ; when, of course, I should take my chance of his assent or refusal. So I suffered the brig to veer away out of sight without speaking to the captain about her, or even appearing to again heed her after I had come down from aloft.

It was a terribly dull, anxious, weary time ; I am speaking of those two uneventful days. The hot breeze had drawn abeam, and blew feverishly under a cloudless sky that was a dazzle of brass all about the sun from morn till evening. We showed royals and a fore-topmast-studdingsail to it, and drove along over the smooth plain with half a fathom's height of foam at the cutwater, and a spin and hurry of snow alongside that made the eyes which watched it reel. I entered the day's work and the necessary observations, and so forth, in the log-book in compliance with the captain's request. He was delighted with my handwriting, sat contemplating it with his un-winking gaze for some considerable time, as though it were a picture, and then, drawing a deep breath, exclaimed : 'There's no question but that eddication's a first-class article. Look at your writing alongside of mine, and at mine alongside of Chicken's. Chicken and me was brought up in the same college—a ship's forecastle, and so far from standing amazed at my own fist and that there spelling,

I'm only astonished that I'm able to read or write at all.'

However, though he broke forth thus, he fell silent, and remained so afterwards, became, indeed, extraordinarily meditative, and at meal-times scarcely opened his lips, though his stare grew more deliberate in proportion as his reserve increased, until it came at last to his never taking his eyes off one or the other of us. Again and again Miss Temple would say to me that she was certain he had something on his mind, and she looked frightened as she theorised upon his secret. Sometimes, when on deck, I would observe him standing at the rail, gazing seaward, and talking to himself, frequently snapping his fingers, whipping round, as though suddenly conscious that he had talked aloud, then starting off in a short, restless, unsteady walk, coming to an abrupt halt to again mutter and to snap his fingers with the air of one labouring to form a resolution.

It was on the afternoon of the second day of those two about which I have spoken, and it was drawing on to six o'clock, four bells of the first dog-watch. The captain had been on deck since four, and for the last twenty minutes he had been standing a little to the right of the fellow who was steering, eyeing me with an intentness that had a long time before become embarrassing, and I may say distressing. Whenever I turned my head towards him, I found his gaze fixed upon me. Miss Temple and I were seated too near him to admit of our commenting upon the singular regard that he was bestowing upon me. She contrived to whisper, however, that she was certain his secret, whatever it was, was slowly rising from the depths of his soul to the surface of his mind.

'I seem to find a change in the man's face,' she said under her breath. 'Let us walk, Mr. Dugdale. Such scrutiny as that is un-bearable.'

As she spoke, four bells were struck forward. Mr. Lush, who was leaning against his windlass end, knocked the ashes out of his pipe and slowly came aft to relieve the deck. I rose to walk with Miss Temple as she had proposed. Captain Braine called my name. He met me as I approached him, and said : 'I want to have a talk with you in my cabin.'

There was something in his manner that alarmed me. How shall I express it? An air of uneasy exultation, as of a mind proud of the achievement of a resolution at which the secret instincts tremble. For a moment I hung in the wind, strongly reluctant to box myself up alone, unarmed as I was, with a man whose insanity, to call it so, seemed stronger in him at this moment than I had ever before observed it. But the carpenter had now gained the poop; and the captain, on seeing him, instantly walked to the companion, down which he went to midway the ladder, and there stood waiting for me to follow him.

Tut, thought I, surely I am more than his match in strength, and I am on my guard! As I put my foot on the ladder—the captain descending on seeing me coming—I paused to lean over the cover and say to Miss Temple:

'If you will remain on deck, I shall be able to get away from him if he should prove tedious, by telling him that I have you to look after.'

'What do you imagine he wishes to say?' she exclaimed with a face of alarm that came very near to consternation.

I could only answer with a helpless shrug of the shoulders, and the next minute I had entered Captain Braine's cabin.

'Pray sit you down,' said he. He pulled off his straw hat and sent it wheeling through the air into a corner, as though it were a boomerang, and fell to drying his perspiring face upon a large pocket-handkerchief; then folding his arms tightly across his breast, and crooking his right knee whilst he dropped his chin somewhat, he stood gazing at me under the shadow of his very heavy eyebrows with a steadfastness I could only compare to the stare of a cat's eye.

'Well, Captain Braine,' said I in an off-hand way, though I watched him with the narrowness of a man who goes in fear, 'what now is it that I am to hear from you? Do you propose to ask me more questions on navigation and seamanship?'

'Mr. Dugdale,' he exclaimed, speaking very slowly, though the excitement that worked in him rendered his voice deep and unusually clear and loud, 'I have come to the conclusion that you are a gentleman very well able to sarve me, and by sarving me to sarve yourself. I've been a-turning of it over in all hours of the day and a good many hours in the night, too, since the moment when ye first stepped over the side, and I've resolved to take ye into my confidence.'

He nodded, and stood looking at me without speech for a few moments; then seated himself near me and leaned forwards with a forefinger upon his thumb in a posture of computing.

'It was in the year 1831,' he began, 'that I was third-mate aboard of a ship called the *Ocean Monarch*. We sailed from London with a cargo of mixed goods, bound to the port of Callao. Nothing happened till we was well round to the west'ards of Cape Horn, when the ship was set afire by the live cinders of the cabin stove burning through the deck. The cargo was of an inflammable kind. In less than two hours the vessel was in a blaze from stem to starn, by which time we had got the boats over, and lay at a distance waiting for her to disappear. There was two boats, the long-boat and a jolly-boat. The longboat was a middling big consarn, and most of the men went in her along with the captain, a man named Matthews, and the second mate, a foreign chap named Falck. In our boat was the chief mate, Mr. Ruddiman, myself, two sailors, and a couple of young apprentices.

We was badly stocked with water and food; and after the *Ocean Monarch* had foundered, Captain Matthews sings out to Mr. Ruddiman to keep company. But it wasn't to be done. The long-boat ran away from us, and then she hove-to and took us in tow; but there came on a bit of a sea, and the line parted, and next morning we was alone.'

He paused.

'I am closely following you,' said I, fancying I perceived in his face a suspicion of inattention in me, and wondering what on earth his story was going to lead to. He stood up, and folding his arms in the first attitude he had adopted, proceeded, his voice deep and clear.

'It came on to blow hard from the south-'ard and east'ard, and we had to up hellum and run before the seas for our lives. This went on for three or four days, till Mr. Ruddiman reckoned that we was blowed pretty nigh half-way across to the Marquesas. It then fell a stark calm, and we lay roasting under a broiling sun with no fresh water in the boat, and nothing to eat but a handful of mouldy fragments of biscuit in the bottom of a bag that had been soaked with spray o'er

and o'er again.   One of the apprentices went
mad, and jumped overboard, and was
drownded.   We was too weak to help him ;
besides, ne'er a one of us but thought him well
off in that cool water, leaving thirst and hunger
behind him, and sinking into a deep sleep, as it
might be.   Then the other apprentice was took
bad, and died in a fit of retching, and we put
him over the side.   When daylight broke on the
morning following that job, we saw one of the
sailors dead in the bottom of the boat.   T'other
was the sicklier man of the two, yet he hung
out, sir, and lived for three days.   We kept
his body.'

His deep tones ceased, and he stared at
me.   Just a story of a bad shipwreck, thought
I, so far.

'There came a light breeze from the east-
'ard,' he continued after a little pause ; 'but
neither Mr. Ruddiman nor me had the strength
of a kitten in our arms, and we let the boat
drive, waiting for death.   I thought it had
come that same afternoon, and on top of
the sensation followed a fit, I allow, for I recollect no more, till on opening my eyes I
found myself in a hammock in the 'tweendecks
of a little ship.   The craft was a small Spanish

vessel, called the *Rosario*. She had floated
into sight of our boat, and there was just
enough strength left in Mr. Ruddiman to
enable him to flourish his handkerchief so as
they might see the boat had something alive
in her. Ne'er a soul aboard spoke a syllable
of English, and neither Mr. Ruddiman nor me
understood a word of Spanish. We couldn't
even get to larn where the brigantine was bound
to, or where she hailed from. We conversed with the crew in signs all the same as
though we had been cast away among savages.
We was both hearty men in those days, and
it wasn't long afore we had picked up what
we had let fall during our ramble in the boat.
Well, the course the vessel made was something to the south'ard o' west, and I took it
we were heading for an Australian port; but
though I'd make motions, and draw with a
piece of chalk on the deck, I'd never get
more'n a stare, and a shake of the head and
a grin, and a shrug of the shoulders, for an
answer. In fact, it was like being sent adrift
along with a company of monkeys.'

He dried his face again, took his seat as
before, and leaned towards me in his former
computing posture with his eyes glued to my

face. The singularity of their habitual expression was now greatly heightened by a look
of wildness, which I attributed in a measure
to the emotions kindled in him by this recital
of past and dreadful sufferings. I sat as though
engrossed by his story ; but I had an eye for
every movement in him as well as for his
face.

'It came on to blow a gale of wind one
night after we had been aboard the brigantine
about a fortnight. They were a poor lot of
sailors in the vessel, and so many as to be in
one another's road. They got the little ship
in the trough, somehow, under more sail than
she could stand up to ; the main-topmast
went ; it brought down the fore-topmast,
which wrecked the bowsprit and jib-boom.
The Spaniards ran about like madmen, some
of them crossing themselves, and praying about
the decks ; others bawling in a manner to
terrify all hands, though I can't tell ye what
was said ; the ship was in a horrible mess with
wreckage, which nobody attempted to clear
away. It blew very hard, and the seas were
bursting in smoke over the brigantine, that lay
unmanageable. At last the boatswain of her,
holding a sounding-rod in his hand, yelled out

something, and there was a rush for the boats stowed amidships. They were so crazy with fear they hardly knew how to swing 'em over the side. Ruddiman says to me : " I shall stick to the ship. If those boats are not swamped, they'll blow away, and her people'll starve, and our late job in that line is quite enough for me." I said I would stick by the ship, too, and we stood watching whilst the Spaniards got their boats over. It was luck, and not management, that set the little craft afloat. The captain roaring out, made signs to us to come; but we, pointing to the sea, made motions to signify that they would be capsized and shook our heads. They were mad with fright, and weren't going to stay to argue, and in twos and threes at a time they sprang into the boats like rats; and whether they took food and water with them I can't tell ye ; but this I know, that within twenty minutes of the Spanish bo'sun's singing out, the two boats had disappeared, and Mr. Ruddiman and me were alone.'

He rose as he said this, and fell to pacing the cabin floor in silence, with his head drooped, and his arms hanging up and down like pump handles.

'A very interesting story, captain, so far as it goes,' said I, shifting a bit on my seat, as though I supposed that the end was not far off now. 'Of course you were taken off by some passing vessel?'

He made no reply to this, nor, indeed, seemed to heed me. After several turns, he stopped, and looked me in the face, and continued to stare with a knitted brow, as though he were returning to his first resolution to communicate his secret with an effort that fell little short of mental anguish. He came slowly to his chair, and started afresh.

'We sounded the well, and presently discovered that the water she was taking in drained through the decks, and that she was tight enough in her bottom; and we reckoned that if we could get her out of the trough, she'd live buoyant; so we searched for the carpenter's chest, and found it, and let fly at the raffle with a chopper apiece, and after a bit, cleared the vessel of the wrecked spars and muddle, and got her to look up to it, and she made middling good weather, breasting it prettily under a tarpaulin seized in the weather main rigging. The gale blew itself out after twenty-four hours, and the wind shifted into the east'ards. We let drop the foresail; there was no more canvas on her to set, with the head of the mast gone, and with it the peak halliards and the sail in rags. Our notion was to head for the Sandwich Islands, for we stood by so doing to fall in with a whaler, and failing help of that sort there was civilisation over at Hawaii; but t'others of the Polynesian rocks were mostly cannibal islands, we believed, and we were for giving them a wide berth. Yet we could do nothing but blow before it. *That* you'll understand, Mr. Dugdale?'

'Quite,' said I.

'It came on thick,' he continued, speaking with intensity and in an utterance deep, clear, and loud, 'with a bit of a swell from the east'ards and a fresh wind singing over it. I was at the hellum in the afternoon, and Ruddiman lay asleep close against the companion hatch. I was drowsy for want of rest, and there was sleep enough in my eyes to make me see very ill. Suddenly looking ahead, I caught sight of a sort of whitish shadow, and even whilst I was staring at it, wondering whether it was vapour or white water, it took shape as a low coral island with clumps of trees here and there and a small rise of greenish land amidships of it. I put the hellum hard over, and called to Ruddiman, who jumps up and takes a look. " A dead lee-shore, Braine," says he ; " what's to be done? There's no clawing off under this canvas." What *was* to be done? The land lay in a stretch of reef right along our beam, with the brigantine's head falling off again to the drag of the foresail, spite of the hellum being hard down. In less than twenty minutes she struck, was took by the swell, and drove hard aground, and lay fixed on her bilge with her deck aslope to the beach that was within an easy jump from the rail.'

He broke off, and went in a restless, feverish way to the table and unlocked and drew out a drawer, looked at something within, then shut the drawer with a convulsive movement of the arm and turned the key. I was now heartily wishing he would make an end. Down to this, the tale was just a commonplace narrative of marine suffering, scarcely reclaimed from insipidity by the singularity of the figure that recited it. But that was not quite it. I was under a constant fear of the next piece of behaviour he might exhibit, and my alarm was considerably increased by the air of mystery with which he had examined the drawer and hurriedly closed it, as though to satisfy himself that the weapon he had lodged there was still in its place. Having locked the drawer, he stood thinking a little, then taking up his Bible from the table, he approached me with it.

'Mr. Dugdale,' he exclaimed, 'before I can go on, I must have ye kiss this here book to an oath. Take it!' he cried with a sudden fierceness; 'hold it, and now follow me.'

'Stop a minute,' I said; 'you are telling me a story that I have really no particular desire to hear. You have no right to exact an oath from me upon a matter that I cannot possibly be in the smallest degree interested in.'

'It's to come,' said he in a raven note; 'ye shall be interested afore long. Take the oath, sir,' he added with a dark look.

'But what oath, man, what oath is it that I am to take?'

'That as the Lord is now a-listening to ye, you will never divulge to mortal creature the secret I'm agoing to tell ye, so help you God:

and if you break your oath, may ye be struck dead at the moment of it, and your soul chased to the very gates of hell. So help ye God, again!'

I looked at him with astonishment and fear. No pen could express his manner as he pronounced these words—the dull fire that entered his eyes and seemed to enlarge them yet, the solemn note his deep and trembling, yet distinctly clear voice took—his mien of command that had the force of a menace in it as he stood upreared before me, his nostrils wide, his face a dingy sallow, one arm thrusting the little volume at me, the other hanging at his side with the fingers clenched.

'I dare not take that oath,' said I, after a little spell of thinking, with every nerve in me tight-strung, so to speak, in readiness to defend myself should he attack me. 'Miss Temple will certainly inquire what our talk has been about; I will not undertake to be silent to her, sir. Keep your secret. It is not too late. Your narrative is one of shipwreck, and so far there is nothing in it to betray.'

With that I rose.

'Stop!' he exclaimed; 'you may tell the lady. There need be no objection. I see how it lies betwixt you and her, and I'm not so onreasonable as to reckon she'll never be able to coax it out of ye. No. Your interests'll be hers, and of course she goes along with us. 'Tis my crew I'm thinking of.'

I was horribly puzzled. At the same time curiosity was growing in me; and with the swiftness of thought I reflected that whether I had his secret or not it would be all the same; he was most assuredly a madman in this direction, anyhow, if not in others; and it could be nothing more than some insane fancy which he had it in his head to impart, and which might be worth hearing if only for the sake of recalling it as an incident of this adventure when Miss Temple and I should have got away from the barque.

'Mr. Dugdale, you will swear, sir,' he exclaimed.

'Very well,' said I; 'but put it a little more mildly, please. Leave out the gates of hell, for instance; or see—suffer me to swear in my own way. Give me that book.'

I observed that his hand was trembling violently as I took the volume from him.

'I swear,' I said, 'to keep secret from all mortal persons in this world, saving Miss

Temple, whatever it is your intention now to tell me. So help me God,' and I put the book to my lips. 'That oath excludes your crew,' I added, ' and I hope you're satisfied?'

His face took a little complexion of life, and he almost smiled.

' It'll do—oh yes, it'll do,' he exclaimed. 'I knew I could count upon you. Now then for it.'

He resumed his seat, and leaning towards me with his unwinking eyes fixed upon my face as usual, he proceeded thus.

CHAPTER XXX

'Mr. Ruddiman and I got ashore and walked a little way up the beach, to see what sort of spot we had been cast away on. It was a small island, betwixt two and three miles long, and about a mile wide in the middle of it. There were no natives to be seen. We might be sure that it was uninhabited. There was nothing to eat upon it, and though we spent the hours till it came on dark in searching for fresh water, we found none. This made us resolve to land all we could out of the brigantine when daylight should arrive. The weather cleared at midnight, the stars shone, and the sea smoothed down with a light swell from the north-west, which the trend of the reef shouldered off and left the water about the stranded craft calm. As soon as daylight came we got aboard, and rigged a whip on the fore-yardarm, and by noon we had landed

provisions enough, along with fresh water and
wines and spirits in jars, to last us two men
for three months; but that didn't satisfy us.
There was no other land in sight all round the
horizon; we were without a boat; and though,
if the vessel broke up, we had made up our
minds to turn to and save as much of her as
we could handle that might wash ashore, so as
to have the materials for a raft at hand if it
should come to it, we hadn't the heart to talk
of such a thing then, in the middle of that
wide ocean, with such a sun as was shining
over our heads all day, and the sure chance
of the first of any squall or bit of dirty
weather that might come along adrowning of
us. So we continued to break out all we
could come at. We worked our way out of
the hold into the lazarette, and after we had
made a trifle of clearance there, we came across
three chests heavily padlocked and clamped
with iron. "What's here?" says Mr. Ruddiman. "If these ain't treasure-chests like to
what the Spanish marchants sends away gold
in along the coast my eyes ain't mates," he
says. He went away to the carpenter's chest,
and returned with a crow and a big hammer,
and let fly at one of the padlocks, and struck

a staple off short.   We lifted the lid, and found
the chest full of Spanish pieces of gold.   The
other two was the same, full up with minted
gold ; and we reckoned that in all three
chests there couldn't be less in the value of
English money than a hundred and eighty to
two hundred thousand pounds !   It wasn't
to be handled in the chests ; so we made
parcels of it in canvas wrappers ; and by the
time the dusk drew down, we had landed
every farden of it.'

Once more he broke off and went to the
drawer.   I watched him with profound
anxiety, incapable of imagining what he was
about to produce, and collecting all my facul-
ties, so to speak, ready for whatever was to
come.   He took from the drawer, however,
nothing more alarming than a piece of folded
parchment, round which some green tape was
tied.   This he opened with trembling hands,
smoothed out the sheet of parchment upon the
table, and invited me to approach.   The outline, formed of thick strokes of ink, represented an island.   Its shape had something of
the look of a bottle with the neck of it broken
away.   It lay due north and south according
to the points of the compass marked by hand

upon the parchment; and towards the north
end of it, on the eastern side, there was a
somewhat spacious indent, signifying, as I supposed, a lagoon.   Over the face of this outline
were a number of crosses irregularly dotted
about to express vegetation.   In the centre of
the lagoon was a black spot like a little blot
of ink, with an arrow pointing from it to
another little blot in the heart of the island
bearing due east from the mark in the indent
or lagoon.   In the corner of the sheet of
parchment were written in a bold hand the
figures, Long. 120° 3' W.; Lat. 33° 6' S.

'This,' said he, in a voice vibratory with
excitement and emotion, 'is the island.'   I
inclined my head.   'You see how it lies, sir,'
he continued, pointing with a shaking forefinger to the latitude and longitude of the
place in the corner.   'Easter Island bears due
north-east from it.   That will be the nearest
land.   Supposing you start from Valparaiso,
a due west-by-south course would run you
stem on to the reef.'

I waited for him to proceed.   He drew
away by a step, that he might keep his eyes
upon my face, whilst he continued to hold his

trembling forefinger pressed down upon his little chart.

'We agreed to bury the gold,' he said ; 'to hide it somewhere where we should be easily able to find it when we came to look for it, if so be as providence should ever allow us to come off with our lives from this destitute reef. D'ye see this hollow, Mr. Dugdale ? '

'A lagoon, I suppose ? ' said I.

'Yes. This here mark amidships of it '— he turned his dead black eyes upon the chart —'signifies a coral pillar about twice as thick as my mainmast, rising out of the water to about fourteen foot. We reckoned that there was no force in nature outside an airthquake to level such a shaft as that, and Mr. Ruddiman and me took it for a mark. We landed the brigantine's compass, and having hit on a clump of trees, found they bore east three-quarters south from that there coral pillar. We fixed upon a tree, and after trying again and again, made it exactly two hundred and eight paces from the wash of the water in the curve of the lagoon. There we buried the money, sir.'

'And there it is now, I suppose ? ' said I.

'Hard upon two hundred thousand

pounds,' he exclaimed, letting the words drop from his lips as though they were of lead. 'Think of it, sir.'

He folded up the sheet of parchment, always with a very trembling hand, replaced it in the drawer, which he locked; and then, after steadfastly gazing at me for some little while, an expression of energy entered his face, and he seemed to quicken from his eyes to his very toes.

'All that money is mine,' said he, 'and I want you to help me recover it.'

'I!'

'Yes, you, Mr. Dugdale. You and me'll do it between us. And I'll tell ye how, if you'll listen'.——

'But, my dear sir,' I exclaimed, 'I suppose you recollect that you are under a solemn promise to Miss Temple and myself to transfer us to the first homeward-bound ship we meet.'

'I can't help that,' he cried with a hint of ferocity in his manner. 'There's this here fortune to be recovered first. After we've got it, home won't be fur off.'

Come, thought I, I must be cool and apparently careless.

'It is very good of you, Captain Braine,

to wish me to participate in this treasure ; but really, my dear sir, I have no title to any portion of it ; besides, I am a man of independent means, and what I possess is quite as much as I require.'

'Ye'll not refuse it when ye see it,' he exclaimed. 'Money's money ; and in this here world, where money signifies everything, —love, happiness, pleasure, everything you can name—who's the man that's agoing to tell me he can get too much of it ? '

'But you haven't completed your story,' said I, strenuously endeavouring to look as though I believed in every word of the mad trash he had been communicating.

'As much as is necessary,' said he. 'I want to come to business, sir. I could keep you listening for hours whilst I told ye of our life aboard that island, how the brigantine went to pieces, how one day Mr. Ruddiman went for a swim in the lagoon, and how the cramp or some fit took him, and he sunk with me a-looking on, being no swimmer, and incapable of giving him any help.'

'And how long were you on the island ? ' said I.

'Four months and three days. It was

one morning that I crawled from the little hut
we had built ourselves out of some of the
brigantine's wreckage that had drifted ashore,
and saw a small man-of-war with her tops'l
aback just off the island. She was a Yankee
surveying craft, and a boat was coming off
when I first see her. They took me aboard,
and landed me at Valparaiso two months later.
But all that's got nothing to do with what I
want to talk to ye about. I've got now to recover this money, and I mean to have it, and
you'll help me to get it, Mr. Dugdale.'

'But why have you waited all this time
before setting about to recover this treasure?'
said I.

'I never had a chance of doing it afore,'
he replied ; 'but it's come now, and I don't
mean to lose it.'

'What is your scheme?'

'As easy,' he cried, 'as the digging up of
the money'll be. I shall head straight away
for Rio, and there discharge all my crew,
then take in a few runners to navigate the
vessel to the Sandwich Islands, where I'll ship
a small company of Kanakas, just as many
as'll help us to sail the *Lady Blanche* to my
island. I shan't fear *them*. Kanakas ain't

Europeans ; they're as simple as babies ; and we can do a deal that they'll never dream of taking notice of.'

I listened with a degree of astonishment and consternation it was impossible for me to conceal in my face ; yet I managed to preserve a steady voice.

'But you have a cargo consigned to Port Louis, I presume ?' said I. 'You don't mean to run away with this ship, do you ? for that would be an act of piracy punishable with the gallows, as I suppose you know ?'

He eyed me steadily and squarely.

'I don't mean to run away with this ship,' he answered ; 'I know my owners, and what they'll think. It'll be a deviation that ain't going to interfere with the ultimate delivery of my cargo at Port Louis, and I don't suppose it'll take me much time to fix upon a sum that'll make my owners very well pleased with the delay, and quite willing that I should do it again on the same tarms.'

'But why do you desire to bring me into this business ?' I exclaimed, startled by the intelligence I found in this last answer of his.

'Because I can trust ye. You're a gentleman, and you'll be satisfied with the share

we'll settle upon. Where am I to find a
sailor capable of helping me to navigate this
ship that I could feel any confidence in, that
I could talk to about this here gold with the
sartinty that he wouldn't play me some
devilish trick ? *Can't* ye see my position, Mr.
Dugdale ? ' he cried with a wild almost
pathetic air of eagerness and pleading. ' I
can't work out such a traverse as this alone.
I must have somebody alongside of me that I
can confide in. Once the money's aboard, we
can rid ourselves of the Kanaka crew, and
ship a company of white men for the run to
the Mauritius. The gold'll be aboard, and
it'll be my secret and yourn.'

Though I never doubted for a moment
that all this was the emission of some mad,
fixed humour, I was yet willing to go on
questioning him as if I was interested,
partly that he might think me sincere in my
profession of belief in his tale, and partly that
I might plumb his intentions to the very
bottom ; for it was certain that, lie or no lie,
his fancy of buried treasure was a profound
reality to his poor brains, and that it would
influence him, as though it were the truth, to
heaven alone knew what issue of hardship

and fatefulness and even destruction to Miss Temple and me.

'I presume,' said I, assuming an off-hand manner, 'that your men have signed for the run to Port Louis and back?'

'Well, sir?'

'How are you going to get rid of them at Rio?'

'Half of them will run, and the rest I shall know how to start.'

'But what excuse will you have for putting into Rio?'

'Want of a chief mate,' he answered, in a deep sepulchral voice.

This threw me all aback again, and thoroughly confounded me. Indeed, I was well enough acquainted with the sea to guess that he was within the truth when he spoke of an easy quittance of the crew at Rio; and assuredly in the want of a chief mate he could find a reason for heading to that South American port, against which it would be impossible for his sailors to find anything to urge, supposing, a thing not to be taken into account, that they had it in their power to insist upon his sailing straight for Mauritius.

But even as I sat looking at him in an interval of silence that fell upon us, a thought entered my head that transformed what was just now a dark, most sinister menace, into a bright prospect of deliverance. As matters stood—particularly now that I had his so-called secret—I could not flatter myself that he would suffer me to leave his ship for a homeward-bound craft, or even for the *Countess Ida* herself, if we should heave her into sight. Consequently, my best, perhaps the only, chance for myself and the girl who looked to me for protection and safety must lie in this madman making for a near port, where it would be strange indeed if I did not find a swift opportunity of getting ashore with Miss Temple. I saw by the expression in his own face that he instantly observed the change in mine. He extended his hand.

'Mr. Dugdale, you will entertain it? I see it grows upon ye.'

'It is a mighty unexpected proposal,' said I, giving him my fingers to hold. 'I don't like the scheme it involves of running away with the ship—the deviation, as you term it, which to my mind is a piratical proceeding. But if you will sign a document to the effect that I acted under compulsion, that I was in your power, and obliged to go with you in consequence of your refusal to transfer me to another ship—if, in short, you will draw up some instrument signed by yourself and witnessed by Miss Temple that may help to absolve me from all complicity in this so-termed deviation, I will consent to accompany you to your island. But I must also know what share I am to expect?'

'A third,' he cried feverishly. 'I'll put that down in writing, too, on a separate piece of paper. As to t'other document, draw it up yourself, and I'll copy it and put my name to it, for I han't got the language for such a job.' He paused, and then said, 'Is it settled?'

'It will be settled,' I answered, 'when those two formal documents are made · out and signed.'

'That can be done at once,' he cried, with profound excitement working in every limb of him, and agitating his face into many sin- · gular twitchings and almost convulsive dila- · tations of the sockets of his eyes.

'Give me leave to think a little,' said I. 'I will have a talk with Miss Temple and settle with her the terms of the absolving letter you are to write and sign.'

'How long will it take ye?' he asked with painful anxiety.

'I shall hope to be ready for you before noon to-morrow,' I replied.

'All right,' said he; 'the moment it *is* settled I'll change my course.'

I took his track-chart and opened it, and with a pair of compasses that lay on the table measured the distance betwixt the point at which we had arrived at noon and Rio. Roughly speaking, and allowing an average of a hundred and fifty miles a day to the barque, I computed that the run would occupy between ten and twelve days.

'What are ye looking for?' he asked suspiciously.

'To see how far Rio is from us,' I answered.

'Well, and what d'ye make it?'

'Call it fifteen hundred miles,' I responded. He nodded in a sort of cunning emphatic way. 'Nothing remains to be said, I think?' said I, making a step to the door.

'Only this,' said he. 'I *was* thinking of asking ye to keep my lookout, acting, as you

will be, as my chief mate, but on consideration I believe it'll be best to wait till we've
got a new crew afore ye take that duty. Not
that the men could object to my calling into
Rio on the grounds that you're aboard and
are good enough as a navigator to sarve my
turn ; because they reckon that you're to be
transhipped along with the lady at the first
opportunity. But it'll be safest, I allow, for
you to remain as ye are this side of Rio.'

'Very well,' said I ; 'but I can continue
to take observations if you like.'

'Oh yes ; there can be no harm in that,'
he answered.

I opened the door.

'Mr. Dugdale,' he exclaimed, softening his
voice into a hoarse whisper with a sudden
expression of real insanity in the gloomy,
almost threatening look he fastened upon me,
'ye'll recollect the oath you've taken, if you
please.'

'Captain Braine,' I replied with an assumption of haughtiness, 'I am a gentleman first of
all, and my oath merely follows ; ' and slightly
bowing, I closed the door upon him.

By this time it was nearly dark. I had
scarcely noticed the drawing down of the

evening whilst in the captain's cabin, so closely
had my attention been attached to him and
his words. Indeed, the man had detained
me an hour with his talk, owing to his
pausings and silent intervals of staring;
though the substance of his speech and our
conversation could have been easily packed
into a quarter that time. I went half-way up
the companion steps, but feeling thirsty, descended again to drink from a jug that stood
upon a swinging tray. Whilst I filled the
glass, my eye at the moment happening to be
idly bent aft, I observed the door of the cabin
adjoining that of Captain Braine's to open
and a man's head showed. It instantly van-
ished. It was too gloomy to allow me to
make sure. However, next moment the
young fellow Wilkins came out, no doubt
guessing that I had seen him, and that he
had therefore better show himself honestly.

I was somewhat startled by the apparition,
wondering if the fellow had been in the berth
throughout our talk, for if so, it was not to
be questioned but that he had overheard every
syllable, for there was nothing between the
cabins but a wooden bulkhead, and the
captain's utterance had been singularly clear,

deep, and loud. But a moment's reflection convinced me that even if he had heard everything, his knowledge (supposing he carried the news forward) would only help to persuade the men that Captain Braine was a madman, and facilitate any efforts I might have to make to deliver myself and Miss Temple from this situation, should Braine's craziness increase and his lunatic imagination take a new turn. So, that the fellow might not think that I took any special notice of his coming out of that cabin, I asked him in a careless way when supper would be ready. He answered that he was now going to lay the table; and without further words I went on deck.

It was a hot and lovely evening, with a range of mountainous but fine-weather clouds in the west, whose heads swelled in scarlet to the fires of the sun sinking into the sea behind them. In the east the shadow was of a deep liquid blue, with the low-lying stars already coming into their places. The breeze blew softly off the starboard beam, and the barque, clothed in canvas to the height of her trucks and to the outmost points of her far-reaching studding-sail booms, was floating quietly and softly, like some spirit-shape of ship, through the rich and tender tropic blending of night-dyes and westering lights.

Miss Temple stood at the rail, leaning upon her arms, apparently watching the water sliding past. She sprang erect when I pronounced her name.

'I was beginning to fear you would never come on deck again,' she exclaimed as she looked at me with a passionate eagerness of inquiry. 'How long you have been! What could he have found to say to detain you all this while?'

'Softly!' I said, with a glance at old Lush, who was patrolling the forward end of the poop athwartships with his hands deep buried in his breeches' pockets, and with a sulky air in the round of his back and the droop of his head. 'I have heard some strange things. If you are not tired, take my arm, and we will walk a little. We are less likely to be overheard in the open air than if we conversed in the silence of the cabin.'

'You do not look miserable,' she exclaimed. 'I expected to see you emerge with a pale face and alarmed eyes. Now, please tell me everything.'

There was something almost of a caress in her manner of taking my arm, as though she could not suppress some little exhibition of pleasure in having me at her side again. Also she seemed to find relief in the expression on my face. She had been full of dark forebodings, and my light smiling manner instantly soothed her.

I at once started to tell her everything that had passed between Captain Braine and myself. I contrived to recite the skipper's yarn as though I fully believed it, always taking care to sober my voice down to little more than a whisper as we alternately approached the fellow at the wheel and the carpenter at the other end in our pendulum walk. Her fine eyes glowed with astonishment; never did her beauty show with so much perfection to the animation of the wonder, the incredulity, the excitement raised by the narrative I gave her.

'So *that* is his secret?' she exclaimed, drawing a breath like a sigh as I concluded, halting at the rail to gaze at her with a smile. 'I presume now, Mr. Dugdale, that you are satisfied he is mad?'

'Perfectly satisfied.'

'You do not believe a word of his story?'

'Not a syllable of it.'

'And yet it might be true!' said she.

'And even then I would not believe it,' I answered.

'Did he explain how it was that all that gold lay hidden in a poor ship like the Spanish brigand—brig—whatever you call it?' she asked, her curiosity as a woman dominating for a moment all other considerations which might grow out of that yarn.

'No,' said I; 'nor would I inquire. It is giving one's self needless trouble to dissect the fabric of a dream.'

'Poor wretch! But how frightful to be in a ship commanded by a madman! What object has he in telling you this secret?'

'He wants me to help him recover the treasure;' and I then related the man's proposals.

She gazed at me with so much alarm that I imagined her fear had rendered her speechless.

'You tell me,' she cried, 'that you have consented to sail with him to this island of his in—in—the Pacific? Are you as mad as he

is, Mr. Dugdale? Do you forget that I look
to you to protect me and help me to return
home?'

Her eyes sparkled; the colour mounted to
her cheek, her bosom rose and fell to the sudden gust of temper.

'I am surprised that you do not see my
motive,' I exclaimed. 'Of course I feigned
to fall in with his views. My desire is to
get to Rio as soon as possible, and ship with
you thence for England.'

'To Rio? But I'm not going to Rio!'
she cried. 'The captain solemnly promised
to put me on board the first ship going home.
Why did you not insist upon his keeping his
word?' she exclaimed, drawing herself up to
her fullest stature and towering over me with
a flashing stare.

'He'll not tranship us now,' said I. 'I'm
like Caleb Williams. I have his secret, and
he'll not lose sight of me.'

'Oh, what miserable judgment!' she exclaimed. 'You are frightened of him! But
were he ten times madder than he is, I would
compel him to keep his word. Rio indeed!
He shall put us on board the first ship we
meet, and I'll tell him so when I see him.'

'You will do nothing of the kind,' said I. 'If you open your lips or suffer your temper to come between me and any project I have formed, I will wash my hands of all responsibility. I will not lift a finger to help ourselves. He shall carry us whithersoever he pleases.'

'How can you talk to me so heartlessly! I have no friend but you now, and you are turning from me, and making me feel utterly alone.'

'I am so much your friend,' said I, 'that I do not intend you shall alienate me. My judgment is going to serve me better than yours in this dilemma. I know exactly what I am about and what I intend, and you must keep quiet and be obedient to my wishes.'

'Oh, I should abhor you at any other time for talking to me like that!' she exclaimed. 'There was a time—— I shall *not* go to Rio! He has promised to put us on board a ship going home.'

'Miss Temple, you talk intemperately. You are in an unreasonable mood, and I will not converse with you. We will resume the subject by-and-by;' and I half turned, as though to walk off, humming an air betwixt my teeth.

She grasped my arm. 'You must not leave me. I have been long enough alone. I believe you will drive me as crazy as the captain.'

'I will see you safely to England first,' said I, ' and then you shall fall crazy.'

The tears suddenly gushed into her eyes, and she turned seawards to hide her face. I moved away, but before I had measured half-a-dozen paces, her hand was again upon my arm.

'I am sorry,' she said softly, hanging her stately head, ' if I have said anything to vex you.'

'I desire but one end,' said I, ' and that is your safety. To ensure it needs but a little exercise of tact on your part and a resolution to trust me.'

'I do trust you,' she exclaimed ; ' but am I wholly wanting in brains, that you will not suffer me to offer an opinion, nay, even to express a regret? '

'You would be able to do nothing with this mad sailor,' said I. ' Rio is within a fortnight's sail, and our safety depends upon our getting there.'

'A fortnight!' she cried—'another fortnight of this horrible ship!'

'Yes; but England is a long way off from
where we are. Were you to get on board
another vessel, you might be fully as uncomfor-
table as you are here, unless she should prove
a passenger craft with ladies in her. A fortnight more or less could not signify. At
Rio you will be able to purchase such articles
as you immediately need, and there will be a
choice of ships to carry us home in comfort.'

'I believe you are right,' said she, after a
little pause, with something of timidity in the
lift of her eyes to my face. 'I was shocked
and made irritable by alarm. I am sorry, Mr.
Dugdale.'

The answer I was about to make was
checked by Wilkins calling to us from the
companion way that supper was ready.

CHAPTER XXXI

THE FORM OF AGREEMENT

THE captain did not arrive, and we had the table to ourselves. Miss Temple was subdued, and her glances almost wistful. It gave me but little pleasure to humble her, or in any way to triumph over her; but I had made up my mind to be master whilst we were together, and not to spare her feelings in my effort to assert myself; and I may add here that I had determined, if it pleased God to preserve us, to make this noble and beautiful woman my wife. For I was now loving her, but so secretly, that my love was scarce like a passion even to my own reason; and the conclusion I had formed was that the only road to her heart lay behind the armour of her pride, which must be broken down and demolished if ever I was to gain her affection. And sure I was of this too; that she was of that kind of women who need to be bowed by a strong hand into a submissive posture before they can be won.

We spoke very little ; the captain's cabin was not far off, and the knowledge of his being in it held us very taciturn. However, we made amends for our silence after we had supped and regained the deck. She was now to be easily convinced that our best chance of escaping from this barque was for me to fool the captain to the top of his bent, that he might carry us to Rio ; and before long she was even talking cheerfully of our prospects, asking me in a half-laughing way how we were to manage for money when we arrived at Rio, whether I had any friends there, and so on.

'There are my jewels,' she said ; 'but I should be very sorry to part with them.'

'There will be no need to do that,' said I. 'I have a few bank-notes in my pocket which I think may suffice. There is an English consul, I suppose, at Rio, and he will advise us.'

Talk of this kind heartened her wonderfully. It gave her something happy and hopeful to think about ; in fact, before we went below she told me that she now preferred the idea of proceeding to Rio to the old scheme of going aboard a ship bound to England.

' I shall be able to purchase a few comforts,'
she said ; ' whereas I might be transferred to
some horrid little vessel that would occupy
weeks in crawling along the sea, and in all
that time I should be as badly off as I am
now. Do the ladies in South America dress
picturesquely, do you know? I should like
to be romantically attired on my arrival home.
How my dearest mother would stare ! What
colour a long Spanish veil and a dress of
singular fashion would give to my story of
our adventures.'

And so she talked.

It was a very calm and lovely night, with
the moon, a few days old, going down in the
west. The breeze held everything silent aloft ;
a murmur as of the raining of a fountain
floated up from alongside as the white body
of the little barque slipped through the darkling waters brimming in a firm black line to
the spangled sky of the horizon. The captain
had arrived on deck at eight, but he kept to
the after-part of the poop, nor once addressed
us, often standing motionless for ten minutes
at a time, till he looked like some ebony
statue at the rail floating softly up and down
against the stars to the delicate curtseying of

his little ship. I seemed to notice, however, yet without giving much heed to the thing, an indisposition on the part of the watch on deck to coil themselves away for their usual fine-weather naps. From time to time, though dimly, there would steal aft a hum of voices from the black shadow upon the deck past the galley. Once a man kindled a phos-phorus match to light his pipe, and a small group of faces showed to the flash of the flame, so to speak, as it soared and sank to the fellow's sucking at it ; but I found nothing in this to arrest my attention saving that I recollect asking Miss Temple to notice the odd effect produced by the coming out of those faces amid the dusk ; for one saw *them* only and no other portion of the men's bodies.

We walked to the companion to leave the deck. I scarcely knew whether or not to call a good-night to the captain, so absorbed in thought did his motionless posture express him. But as Miss Temple put her foot upon the steps, he quietly cried out : 'Are ye going to bed ? '

'Yes, captain,' I answered, 'and we wish you a very good-night.'

'A minute ! ' he sung out, and came to us.

He seemed to peer into Miss Temple's face, that showed as a mere faint glimmer in the starlight, the moon being then sunk, and addressing me, exclaimed in a voice but a little above a whisper: 'I suppose you have told the lady everything, Mr. Dugdale?'

'Yes,' I answered; 'my oath allowed for that, you know.'

'Certainly,' said he. 'It's a grand opportunity for money-getting, mem. The brace of you know more than the wife of my own bosom has any suspicion of. As God's my Saviour, never once have I opened my lips to Mrs. Braine about that there money.'

'I had hoped you would have transferred me to a homeward-bound ship,' said Miss Temple.

'You don't want to be separated from your sweetheart, do you?' he exclaimed.

This was a stroke to utterly silence her. I believe she had spoken from no other motive than to finesse, that the captain might suppose her as sincere in her belief of his story as I was; but this word *sweetheart* was like a blast of lightning. What her face would have exhibited if there had been light enough to see it by, I could only imagine.

'It grows late, captain; good-night,' said
I, pitying her for the confusion and disorder
which I knew she would be under.

'Have you been thinking over the tarms
of that letter we were talking about ? ' said he.

'Yes,' I answered.   'I'll pay your cabin a
visit after breakfast and write it out.'

'Very well, sir.   That and the agreement
about the division of the money too.   I shall
want to shift my hellum for Rio to-morrow.'

He left us, and we descended in silence,
nor did Miss Temple speak a word to me as
we made our way to our gloomy deep-sunk
quarters, excepting to wish me good-night.

I slept well, and rose next morning at
seven to get a bath in the head ; for, as in the
Indiaman, so in this barque, and so, indeed, in
most ships in those days, there was a little
pump fixed in the bows for washing down the
decks of the fore-part of the craft.   It was a
very gay brilliant morning, a fresh breeze
about a point before the starboard beam, and
the *Lady Blanche* was moving through it at a
meteoric pace with her royals and gaff topsail
in, and all else save the flying jib abroad.
The water was of a rich blue, and rolled in
snow ; the violet shadows of swollen steam-

coloured clouds swept over the rolling lines of
the ocean, and by their alternations of the
sunshine made a very prism of the vast,
throbbing disc of the deep. About two miles
astern was a large schooner, staggering along
on a westerly course, so close hauled that she
seemed to look into the very eye of the wind
and plunging bow under with a constant
boiling of foam all about her head. By the
time I had taken my bath she was a mere chip
of white on the windy blue over our weather
quarter.

There were a few sailors cleaning up about
the decks, and as I passed them on the road
to the cabin, I could not fail to observe that
they eyed me with a degree of attention I had
never before noticed in them. Their looks
were full of curiosity, with something almost
of impudence in the bold stare of one or two
of them. What, I reflected, can this signify
but that the fellow Wilkins overheard everything that passed between the captain and me,
and has carried the news into the forecastle?
So much the better, I thought; for should the
captain come to guess that the men had his
secret, the suspicion must harden him in his

E 2

insane resolve to carry the barque forthwith
to Rio to get rid of his crew.

When Miss Temple came out of her berth
there was a momentary touch of bashfulness
and even of confusion in her manner ; then
a laughing expression flashed into her eye.
As we repaired to the cabin we exchanged
some commonplaces about the weather. She
warmed up a little when I spoke of the noble
breeze and of the splendid pace of the barque,
and assured her that the most distant port in
the world could never be far off to people
aboard such a clipper keel as this. The
captain joined us at the breakfast table. I
thought he looked unusually haggard and
pale, appearing as a man might after a long
spell of bitter mental conflict. His eyes
seemed preternaturally large, and of a duller
and deader black than my recollection found
common in them. He seldom spoke but to
answer the idle conversational questions one
or the other of us put to him. I observed
that he drank thirstily and ate but little, and
that he would occasionally rest his forehead
upon his hand as though to soothe a pain
there Yet lustreless as was his gaze, it was
singularly eager and devouring in its stead-

fastness. He had been on deck since four o'clock, he told us, and had not closed his eyes during the previous four hours of his watch below.

'I get but little sleep now,' said he with a long trembling sigh.

'That schooner astern this morning,' said I, 'looked as if she were bound somewhere Rio way.'

He responded with a dull nod of indifference.

'Were you ever at Rio, Captain Braine?' asked Miss Temple.

'No, mem.'

'I suppose I shall easily find a ship there to carry me home?' said she.

He stared at her and then at me; and then said, looking at her again, 'Don't you mean to go along with him?' indicating me with a sideways jerk of the head.

Her eyes sought mine for counsel.

'It will be a question for you and me to discuss, captain,' said I. 'With all due deference to Miss Temple, it may be you will come to think that the presence of a lady could but encumber us in such a job as we have in hand.'

'Ay, but she has my secret!' said he swiftly and warmly.

'Your secret is mine, and my interests are hers—you know that!' I exclaimed.

'What are the relations between you?' he asked.

A blush overspread Miss Temple's face and her eyes fell.

'Ask me that question presently, captain,' said I, laughing.

He continued to stare slowly at one or the other of us, but remained silent.

Wilkins entered with a pot of coffee. I furtively but attentively surveyed his expressionless veal-like countenance; but I might as well have explored the sole of his foot for hints of what was passing in his mind. He came and went quickly. Indeed, his practice of waiting consisted merely in placing our meals upon the table, and then lingering out upon the quarter-deck within hearing of the captain's voice if he was wanted.

Presently the skipper rose.

'I've made out that document consarning shares,' said he; 'perhaps you might now come with me and con-coct the letter you want me to sign.'

'Very well,' I answered; 'Miss Temple is to witness your signature, and you will allow her to accompany us?'

For answer he gave her one of his astonishing bows, and the three of us went to his cabin. He opened the drawer that contained the chart of his island, and produced a sheet of paper, very oddly scrawled over.

'I made this up last evening,' said he; 'jest see if it'll do, Mr. Dugdale. If so, I'll sign it, and ye can draw me up a copy for my own keeping.'

'Miss Temple will have to witness this too,' said I, 'so I'll read it aloud :

"Barque *Lady Blanche.*

At Sea (*such and such a date*).

I, John Braine, master of the barque *Lady Blanche,* do hereby agree with   Dugdale, Esquire, that in consideration of his serving me as chief-officer for a voyage to an island situate in the South Pacific Ocean, latitude 33° 16′ S. longitude 120° 3′ W., onnamed, but bearing due south-west from Easter Island, distant   ; I say that in consideration of your helping me to navigate this ship to that there island, and from there to Port Louis in the island of Mauritius afterwards, the said John Braine do hereby undertake to give and secure to the said Dugdale, Esquire, by this here instrument as witnessed, one whole and full third of the money now lying buried in the above-said island, whereof the amount, as by calculation allowed, is in Spanish pieces from 180 to 200,000 pounds.

Witness my hand and seal." '

It cost me a prodigious effort to keep my face whilst I read, almost tragical as was the significance of this absurd document to Miss Temple and myself, as forming a condition, so to speak, of the extraordinary adventure fate had put us upon. I durst not look at her for fear of bursting into a laugh. The man's strange eyes were fixed upon me.

'Nothing could be better,' said I. 'Now, sir, if you will kindly sign it—and I will ask you, Miss Temple, to witness it.'

He turned to seat himself; the girl's glance met mine; but heaven knows there was no hint of merriment in *her* face. She was colourless and agitated, though I could perceive that she had a good grip of her emotions. The captain signed his name with a great scratch-

ing noise of his pen, then made way for Miss
Temple, whose hand slightly trembled as she
attached her signature to the precious document.   It was now my turn ; in a few minutes
I had scribbled out a form of letter addressed
to myself guaranteeing me immunity from all
legal perils which might follow upon the
captain's piratical deviation from his voyage.
This also he signed, and Miss Temple afterwards put her name to it as a witness.

'I'll take copies of these,' said I, ' at noon,
after helping you to work out the sights.'

'I beg pardon,' he exclaimed, observing
me to take a step towards the door ; ' I should
be glad to know the relations 'twixt you and
this young lady?   It ain't for inquisitiveness
that I ask.   She has my secret, sir ; ' and he
drew himself erect.

'We were fellow-passengers,' I answered
with a side-look at the girl, whose expression
was one of disgust and distress.

'There's nothing close in that,' said he ;
'I counted upon ye as being sweethearts—
that you was keeping company with her, and
to be married when the chance came, when I
told you there was no objection to your reporting my secret to her.'

'We are sweethearts,' I replied, smiling, and taking the girl's hand; 'and *when* the chance comes along,' I added, faintly accentuating the 'when' for *her* ear only, 'we shall be married, captain, and I shall hope to see you dancing at our wedding and heartily enjoying the entertainment, which it will not need all my third share to furnish forth.'

Miss Temple could not contain herself; she uttered a short hysteric laugh.

'Pity ye couldn't have told me this at once,' exclaimed the captain, regarding me sternly; 'but,' he went on whilst his countenance slightly relaxed, 'there's always sensitiveness in love-making whilst it keeps young. I'm obliged to you, mem, for your visit.'

I opened the door and followed Miss Temple out.

'I am of opinion that he is not so mad as he appears,' said I.

She averted her flushed face somewhat haughtily. No matter, thought I; it is a subject that will keep.

We got under the short awning on the poop and lounged away the morning there. Her good breeding speedily came to her rescue, and our chat was as easy, in a sense,

as ever it could have been aboard the Indiaman—easier, i' faith, by a long chalk! though
it concerned troubles and anxieties which
never could have occurred to us in the
Countess Ida. I observed that Mr. Lush frequently directed his eyes at me as he paced
the weather deck. To my accost he had
satisfied himself with returning a surly ' marning,' and we spoke no more. He seemed
unable to view me attentively enough to
satisfy himself without growing offensive by
staring.

'I hope that fellow,' I whispered to Miss
Temple, ' may not thwart my Rio programme.
Yet I don't see how he could do so. The
barque wants a chiefmate, so the captain
contends. It is no falsehood ; the need would
by all sailors be regarded as an imperative
one. Still, I hate that surly fellow without
exactly knowing why.'

'Do you notice how those men yonder are
constantly looking this way ? '

' Yes. As I have explained to you, Master
Eavesdropper Wilkins has reported all he
heard ; and the Jacks understanding at last
that their skipper is a madman, are wondering
what on earth is going to happen next. They'll

be glad, you'll find, to learn that we're heading
for Rio when the course is changed. They'll
report the skipper as insane, and end our
difficulties out of hand for us.'

'I hope so indeed!' she sighed.

Well, for the rest of the day nothing
happened worth relating. I took an observation with the captain, worked it out in
his cabin, and made draughts of the two
extraordinary documents. When we had
calculated our situation, he went on deck, and
by a tell-tale compass in his cabin I perceived
that he had changed the barque's course.
Simultaneously with this, I heard the men
bracing the yards more forward, and the heel
of the barque slightly sharpened to the increased lateral pressure of the fresh breeze
upon her canvas. I hastened on deck when
I had done my copying to observe the crew's
deportment; but in the manner of the few
men who were about I witnessed nothing to
lead me to suppose that they made anything
of this sudden change of course.

When I told Miss Temple that we were
now heading as close as the wind would let us
lie for the South American port she instantly
grew animated; her eyes brightened, a look

of hope and pleasure entered her face, and
her voice was full of cheerfulness. The captain, on the other hand, grew gloomier as the
day advanced. During his watch on deck
from twelve to four he paced the planks
without any intermission that I was sensible
of, walking nearly always in the same posture,
with his hands clasped behind him and his
head bowed; and with his long black hair,
yellow face, and blue gills he needed nothing
but the dress of a monk to look one, rehears-
ing his part for the cloisters.

Some dinner was taken to him on deck;
but I saw Wilkins afterwards carry the dishes
forward, and the food appeared to me un-
touched. At the supper hour he came to the
table, but neither ate nor drank. During the
greater part of the sitting he kept turning his
eyes first on one and then on the other of
us with a dim sort of strained interrogative
expression in his stare, as though he was
struggling with some degree of suffering to
dislodge an imagination or idea out of a remote
secret cell of his brain and bring it forward
into the clear light of his understanding.
He seemed to find Miss Temple's presence a
restraint. Sometimes, after eyeing me he'd

start as if about to speak, but instantly check himself with a glance at the girl, whilst his face would darken to some mood of irritation and impatience.

Another gloriously fine night followed sunset that day, with a brighter and longer-living moon, and a gushing of breeze that melted through and through one with the delicious coolness that it brushed off the waters and gathered from the dew. The sea throbbed in flashings of foam, which shone with the radiance of moon-touched snow mingled with spangles of the gold and emerald light of the phosphor. There was a pleasant roaring and hissing noise off the weather bow, with merry whistlings aloft, where the full-throated canvas soaring to the main-topgallant yard leaned in pale spaces against the stars, with frequent sweeps of the mastheads to the frisky plungings of the clipper hull upon the head seas.

The carpenter was in charge of the deck. He was standing at the rail abreast of the wheel, when it occurred to me to accost him, that I might gather from his replies what notions had been put into his head by the captain' having changed the course. I had

Miss Temple on my arm, for the deck was
hardly safe for her without some such support.
We went to the binnacle, and I took a peep at
the card, then crossed over to the carpenter.

'Good-evening, Mr. Lush. A rattling
breeze this! Since Rio is our destination,
such a draught as this should put us in the
way of making it smartly, off her course as the
barque is.'

'I suppose you know what we're a-going
there for?' he answered in a gruff tone of
voice, that left me in doubt as to whether he
intended a question or not.

'You are second mate, and of course are
in the captain's confidence. What should I
know that you don't?'

'Ah, what?' he exclaimed, in a voice like
a dog's growl.

Miss Temple slightly pressed my arm, as
though she would have me walk away.

'A vessel like this wants a chief mate,' said
I, 'some one who knows what to do with the
sun and stars.'

'Oh, then, you're acquainted with the
reason why we're going to Rio?' said he in a
tone of such impudent sarcasm, that without
another word I rounded on my heel and led
Miss Temple forward.

'The brute!' I exclaimed. 'But I am rightly served. I have no business to address the surly illiterate baboon.'

'You know that *he* knows you have learnt the captain's motives, if it be true, as you suppose, that Wilkins has repeated to the men what he overheard; why, then, do you feign an ignorance that can only excite the creature's suspicions?'

'Suspicions of what?'

'That you are acting a double part: with the captain for the sake of his buried money, and with the crew for the sake of your safety.'

'You put it shrewdly, and I am fairly hit,' said I. 'I wanted to get at the fellow's mind, if he has any; it did not occur to me for the moment that he would know through Wilkins of what had passed in the cabin. That is to say if he *does* know; for after all, Wilkins may not have overheard everything, and for aught we can tell he may not have repeated a syllable of the little that he managed to collect through that bulkhead. No matter, Miss Temple. A fortnight more, please God, and we shall be able to write the word finis to this passage of our adventures.'

'I shall scarcely know myself again,' she exclaimed cheerfully, whilst she extended her disengaged white hand to the sheen in the air flowing from the stars and scar of moon, 'when I put my rings on once more. What an experience! How improbable, and how consistently possible and horribly absolute!'

And then she asked me how far it was from Rio to London; and we went on chatting and pacing, sometimes coming to a stand at the side to watch some sweep of foaming water roaring off from the blow of the lee bow into the weltering gloom until five bells were struck—half-past ten. She then said she felt chilly, and I took her below. It was a little early for bed, however; besides, the excitement of the day still lingered—the signing and witnessing of the queer documents: the captain's insane dream of a treasure-quest, mad, as we deemed it, at all events: the sense of our speeding now towards a port whence we should be able to take ship and proceed comfortably to England.

I went to the cuddy door and called for Wilkins, and on his arrival told him to put a bottle of the wine that had been brought from the wreck on the table along with some biscuit,

and thus furnished, Miss Temple and I managed
to kill very nearly another hour.   She removed
her hat ; the lamplight streamed fair upon the
marble-like beauty of her face, upon her large,
dark, soft, and glowing eyes, upon her rich
neglected abundant hair.

' Do you remember that night,' I said, ' in
the English Channel, when after the collision
with the Frenchman you came to where I
stood and asked me to explain what had
happened ? '

' I would rather not remember anything
that passed between us on board the Indiaman, Mr. Dugdale,' she replied with a droop
of her long lashes as she spoke.

I gazed at her earnestly ; a single glance
would have enabled her to witness something
of passion in my regard at that instant : I bit
my lip to check what my instincts assured me
would then have been said all too soon, and
looking at my watch exclaimed : ' Hard upon
half-past eleven.'

She rose, and together we descended to
our inhospitable steerage quarters.

CHAPTER XXXII

A TRAGEDY

IIow long it was before I fell asleep I cannot
say. The humming of the wake racing away
close outside was noisy ; the light cargo in the
steerage creaked and strained, and the thump
of the rudder was frequent, and sometimes
startling. I was aroused by a continuous
knocking on the bulkhead. It was pitch-dark,
despite a small sliding dance of stars in the
porthole glass. I thought the knocking was
upon my door, and cried out, 'What is it?'
It did not cease ; and gathering by this time
that it proceeded from the bulkhead that
divided the cabins, I jumped out of my bunk
and beat upon the boards to let Miss Temple
know I heard her.

I called ; but though I caught her voice,
I could not distinguish her utterance. I had
turned in partially clothed, and groping my
way to the door, stepped forth and knocked

F 2

upon her cabin. The handle was touched
and I was sensible that the girl's door was
ajar.

'Are you there, Mr. Dugdale?'

'Yes. What is the matter?'

'Did not you hear a pistol-shot?'

'No,' I cried.

'I am certain a firearm has been discharged,' she exclaimed.

'Stay a bit,' said I. 'I will see if anything
is wrong, and let you know.'

After some groping, I succeeded in lighting the candle in my lantern; and then
slipping on my shoes, I made for the hatch
ladder, which I was able to see by leaving my
cabin door open. I entered the cuddy and
listened. The lamp had been extinguished;
but a sort of spectral illumination of stars and
white water came sifting through the skylight
and the port-holes and the little windows in
the cuddy front, and I was able to determine
the outline of objects. All was right in this
interior, so far as I could tell. I listened; but
not so much as a footfall sounded upon the
upper deck, not a note of human voice or
movement of men forward. The barque was
sweeping through the seas bravely, and the

atmosphere of the cuddy was vibratory with
the resonant cries of the wind up aloft.

I made for the cuddy door and looked
out; nothing stirred on the quarter-deck that
ran pallid into the impenetrable shadow past
the waist. I returned to the companion
steps, which I mounted, and stood in the
hatch a moment or two. There was nobody
on the poop saving the man at the helm. I
stepped over to him and said, ' Where's the
captain ? '

' He's gone below,' he answered; ' he told
me he wouldn't be long.'

' When did he leave the deck ? '

' Seven or eight minutes ago, belike.'

' Did you hear a noise just now that resembled a pistol-shot ? ' I inquired.

' No, sir,' he answered. ' But who's to
hear anything atop of this here shindy of wind
and water ? '

' That's true,' I exclaimed. ' I doubt if
the noise will have meant more than a fall of
something below. It is the lady who heard
the sound, and I've just stepped up to see
what it might mean. It's to be hoped the
captain won't linger. This is not a breeze in
which to leave a ship in charge of her helmsman only.'

And indeed the little craft wanted too much watching on the part of the fellow to suffer him to talk or to permit of my calling off his attention from his duty. I resolved to wait, that there might be some sort of look-out kept whilst the captain stayed below. The breeze had freshened, I thought, since I left the deck; there was a dim windy look, moreover, all away out to starboard; and the barque close hauled was making the wind to come as hard again as it was blowing, in fact, through her thrusting, plunging, nimble manner of looking up into it. The mainsail is too much for her, thought I; it should be furled. There is a staysail or two too many, also; and that top-gallant-sail will have to come in anon, if the look of the sky out yonder means what it threatens.

Five minutes passed, but the captain did not make his appearance. The sound that Miss Temple had heard was beginning to work an ugly fancy in my mind. I stepped aft to the wheel.

'Did the captain tell you why he was going below?'

'No, sir,' was the answer. 'He'd been standing for about a quarter of an hour stock

still ; then he comes soddenly in a sort o' run
to the binnacle, takes a look at the card, and
says : " Keep her as she goes ; nothing off :
see to it ! I shan't be long." That was all.'

At that instant the wind breezed up in a
gust that came in a long howl over the weather
rail, and the little vessel bowed down to it
till the smother alongside looked to be up to
the covering-board.

'No use waiting for the captain,' said I,
made irritable by anxiety ; 'we shall have
the masts out of her if we don't mind our
eye ;' and running forward, I shouted at
the top of my voice : 'Lay aft and haul up
the mainsail !'

In a moment the watch came tumbling
out of the darkness forward. Their manner
of rushing gave me to know that they had
been standing by for the order to shorten sail,
and were wondering why it had not been
delivered sooner.

'Furl it, lads,' I shouted, ' when you've
hauled it up ; but first get your maintopgallant staysail hauled down. I must find out
what has become of the captain.'

Without losing another moment, I ran
into the cuddy and knocked upon the door of

the captain's cabin. No answer was returned.
I knocked again, thundering with my fist;
then tried the handle, and found the door
locked. 'Good God!' thought I, 'the man
has shot himself. *That* will be the meaning
of the sound Miss Temple heard.' As I
turned for a moment, utterly at a loss how to
act, the girl rose through the hatch close to
where I stood. She held in her hand the
lantern I had left alight in my berth.

'What has happened?' she cried.

'I have no notion as yet,' I responded;
'but I fear the captain has shot himself. Let
me take that lantern from you.'

I swiftly hitched it by its laniard to a hook
in a stanchion, noticing as I did so that she
had completely dressed herself.

'Remain here for the present, will you?'
I went on. 'I must go on deck—there is no
one to give orders to the men.'

I ran up the steps, and perceived the
shadowy shapes of the seamen ascending the
shrouds to lay out upon the main yard.

'Who is that there?' I called, observing a
dark figure standing near the main hatch.

'Me—Wilkins, sir.'

'Jump forward, Wilkins,' I shouted, 'and

call Mr. Lush. Tell him I want him aft—that
I'm afraid something serious has happened;
in fact, rout up all hands. We shall be having
to reef down shortly.'

The fellow sped forwards. It had been
no passing gust that had bowed the barque
down, but a real increase in the weight of
wind; and by this time, knowing fairly well
how the gear led, I let go the maintopgallant
halliards, and then ran aft to the mizzen top-
mast staysail halliards, and was dragging with
my single pair of hands upon the downhaul,
when the carpenter came up to me, followed
by the rest of the watch below.

'What's gone wrong?' he said.

'I believe the captain has shot himself.
His cabin door is locked, and we have yet to
discover that he has committed suicide. The
wind freshens, the ship wants watching, and
there is nobody to see to her. Will you take
charge? I'll wait for you in the cabin.'

What expression a light cast upon his
countenance might have shown my news
produced in it I know not; there was a pause
in him, as of sulky astonishment, but he said
nothing. He mounted the poop ladder; and
I entered the cuddy, catching the sound as I

did so of the men on the main yard chorusing
as they triced up the bunt of the sail, along
with a sudden roar from the carpenter to
clew up the main-topgallant-sail and furl it.
The candle end burning in the lantern made
but a wretched light, as you will suppose.
Close beside it, in such radiance as it emitted,
stood Miss Temple, white as stone, and her
eyes wide and luminous with alarm.

'Is the vessel in danger?' she asked.

'Oh dear, no,' I replied; 'the breeze has
freshened considerably, and the men are
shortening sail. But this light is truly
abominable. We shall require to be able to
see clearly presently.' And with that I took
out the candle and lighted the cabin lamp
with it.

'I have been every moment expecting to
see that door open, and *his* figure creep out!'
said Miss Temple, pointing with a shudder,
and without looking, towards the captain's
berth. 'Do you believe he has shot himself?'

'Not a doubt of it. Why should his door
be locked? I should know he has destroyed
himself without being able to make a guess at
his method of doing so, but for your saying
that you heard the report of a pistol.'

'I assuredly heard it, Mr. Dugdale. I was awake. I have not slept since I lay down. The sound was like the crack of a whip over my head.'

Just then the carpenter roared out some fresh orders. The barque, relieved of her mainsail and topgallant-sail, had recovered from her perilous heel, and was thrashing through it with what seemed a stubborn erectness of spar after the recent wild slope of her masts. The sea was rising, and the vessel was beginning to pitch with some spite in the chopping and smiting shear of her clipper bows, from which the surge recoiled in thunder, washing aft in boiling spume with a sound like the fall of the hail and rain of an electric storm. I could tell without needing to look that Mr. Lush's latest order concerned the reefing of the foretopsail. At all events, he had his little ship well in hand, and the whole of the vessel's small crew were on deck to run about to his directions, and there was some comfort to be got out of knowing this.

To satisfy a small doubt that had arisen, I stepped once again over to the captain's cabin and hammered loud and long upon the door, shouting out his name, and then trying the handle ; but to no purpose.

'For what new horrors are we reserved ?' cried Miss Temple. 'Shall we ever escape with our lives? How much has been com- pressed within the last few days: the dead body on the wreck—the drowning of the poor lieutenant—the loss, perhaps, of Mr. Colledge and the sailors in the man-of-war's boat—and now this!' she cried, bringing her hands to her face with a sudden convulsive, tearless sob ; then looking at me she said : 'If Captain Braine has killed himself, what is to follow ?'

'Rio,' I answered. 'I shall carry the ship there straight. Thank God for such know- ledge of navigation as I possess ! I trust the captain may not have killed himself; but if he has done so, it will make for our good. He was a madman, and it was impossible from hour to hour to be sure of his intentions.'

'But, Mr. Dugdale, there will be no head to the ship if the captain be dead. Who, then, is to control the crew—this crew of convicts and mutineers and—and ?'——

'It was a madman who drew that picture,' said I. 'I suspect he is as correct in his description of his crew as in his description of his treasure. The men are without a navigator; they can do nothing without me. If they are true Jacks, they are already sick of the voyage, and will be glad to have a port under their lee, with the promise of a jaunt ashore and fresh articles to sign on another ship's capstan.'

We continued talking thus; presently I heard the seamen chorusing at the foretopsail halliards, and later on the carpenter Lush entered the cabin by the cuddy door.

'She'll be snug at this,' he exclaimed in his gruff voice; 'there's no more weight of wind, and the whole main-topsail won't be too much for her if it don't freshen yet. What's this about the capt'n, sir?'

As he spoke, I observed the glimmering faces of the crew, the whole body of them, saving the fellow at the wheel, crowding to take a peep through the cuddy windows and doorway. I saw Miss Temple glance with terror towards them; but there was nothing more natural than that the fellows should desire to obtain all news of an event that concerned them so closely as the suicide of their captain. I repeated what little I knew to the carpenter, who at once stalked to the captain's door and tried the handle for himself, shaking it viciously.

'I suppose it'll have to be broke open?' he exclaimed, looking round.

'Certainly,' I answered, 'and the sooner the better. This suspense is intolerable.'

'I'll go forrards and get some tools,' he said.

He returned after a few minutes, and two seamen accompanied him, one of them being Joe Wetherly. The others, heedless of all custom, in their devouring curiosity came shouldering one another into the cuddy, thrusting inch by inch to the centre of it, where they stood staring—a wild and rugged group, indeed, in that light; hairy breasts, naked, weather-darkened nervous arms liberally scored with blue devices, bare feet, gleaming eyes, sheath-knives on their hips—I could scarcely wonder that Miss Temple shrank from them, and clung to my side with her hand in my arm! They did not need the character the captain had given them to make her do that!

Lush forced the door of the berth; it flew open to a heavy blow, and I advanced to take a view of the interior, Miss Temple letting go

of my arm with an exclamation, rather choosing to remain alone near the sailors than take
a peep at the horror her imagination bodied
forth. A small bracket lamp was burning
brightly. In the centre of the deck of the
cabin lay the body of Captain Braine. He
was on his breast, his arms were outstretched,
one leg was crooked, as though broken under
the other. A pistol of a pattern somewhat
similar to the one I had discovered in Mr.
Chicken's locker lay beside his right hand.
These details we immediately witnessed; but
we had to look a little before we could distinguish the great stain of blood upon the
square of drugget under the cheek of the poor
creature, and showing in a black line from a
hole on a level with his eye.

'He has shot himself, as you said,' exclaimed the carpenter in a hoarse note, and
backing half a pace to the right.

'Turn him over, Bill,' said Wetherly to the
other sailor.

'Not me! Handle him yourself, Joe.'

Wetherly fell upon a knee, and got the
corpse on its back. After my experience
with the body on the wreck, I should have
deemed myself equal to any sort of ghastly

sight-seeing; but that dead captain's face was more than I could bear, and I was forced to look away and to keep my gaze averted, to rally my nerves from the shock the spectacle had given them.

The crew had come shoving right to the very cabin door, and stood in a crowd, staring open-mouthed with a sort of groaning of exclamations breaking out from amongst them.

'A bad job this, sir,' said Wetherly, looking round to me.

'He'll be stone-dead, I suppose?' said the carpenter.

'O God, yes!' I exclaimed.

The carpenter seemed to wait, as if he expected me to give directions.

'Better get the body into the bunk, Mr. Lush,' said I, 'and cover it up for to-night.'

'Ay, hide it as soon as ye will, Joe,' exclaimed the carpenter; and as he said these words, I observed that he rolled his eyes with an expression in them of keen and thirsty scrutiny over the cabin.

Wetherly and the other man who had entered with him lifted the body, placed it in the bunk, and threw a blanket over it. We then quitted the cabin, leaving the lamp burning, though, I fancy, nobody noticed that but myself; and the carpenter put a little wedge of wood under the door to keep it shut. The sailors slowly walked away out on to the quarter-deck, casting inquisitive glances around them, and at Miss Temple, as they withdrew. The carpenter came to a stand at the table, and turning his surly face upon me, exclaimed in his deep-sea, bad-tempered voice: 'What's to be done now?'

'There's nothing for it,' I answered, 'but to make for the nearest port, and Rio will be that.'

'Ay; but that ain't the question just at present,' he exclaimed. 'What I mean is, what's the discipline agoing to be?'

'Why, of course,' I exclaimed, 'I must render all the assistance I possibly can. If the crew consent, I shall be happy to keep watch and watch with you. In any case, I'll navigate the ship. Very fortunately, I can do so.'

'It'll be a matter for the crew,' said he, talking with his eyes upon the deck and speaking after a pause. 'To-morrow morning will be time enough to settle what's to be

done. I kep' a lookout from eight to twelve
to-night ; and if you'll stand this here middle
watch, I'll be a relieving of ye at four ; and
arter breakfast, giving you time to get some
sleep, I'll call the crew aft, and we'll see what
they've got to say, now there ain't neither
mate nor capt'n left.'

'But you are the mate ; the acting second
mate,' I cried, sensible of an indefinable misgiving that grew rapidly into an emotion of
cold and heart-sickening consternation.

'I tell ye *no*, sir !' he shouted ; 'I'm no
second mate. I signed on as ship's carpenter,
and I've told ye so. Since Mr. Chicken died,
I've been treated by that man there '—he
pointed with a square forefinger to the cabin
door—'worse than any mongrel dog that e'er
a blunderbuss was brought to bear on. *Me* a
second mate ? '   He struck his breast in a sort
of frenzy with his clenched fist and grinned
in my face.

'Very well,' said I, forcing a note of composure into my voice ; 'it is a mere detail of
routine, which we can settle to-morrow, as
you say.'

'All right,' he exclaimed ; and pulling his
skin cap down over his head, he trudged on
his rounded legs out of the cuddy.

'I must go on deck, Miss Temple,' said I.

She was eyeing me, as though bereft of speech, when I addressed her.

'I will accompany you,' she exclaimed.

'No! It is out of the question.'

'Why?' she cried imperiously, with the irritability of dismay and dread in her manner.

'I shall be on deck till four. Such a spell of exposure it will be needless for you to undergo. You are perfectly safe in your cabin.'

'How *dare* you ask me to return to that horrible lonely part of the ship?' she cried, with wrath and alarm brilliant in her eyes.

'Then take some rest upon that locker there.'

'You ask me to remain here *alone* with the dead body close to in that cabin?'

'Miss Temple,' said I firmly, 'if you decline to return to your cabin, you will at least oblige me by staying in this cuddy. I have no time to reason with you. You must obey me, if you please. Give me your hand.' She extended it, and I conducted her to the sofa locker, on which I gently but resolutely compelled her to seat herself. 'You can rest here with perfect safety,' I went on. 'I am astonished that a woman of your spirit should find anything to render you uneasy, in the face of the real difficulties which confront us, in the neighbourhood of a harmless corpse. I can command a view of you and of this interior through that skylight. But you must not come on deck.'

She watched me in a motionless posture with an air of haughty resentment upon her lips, to which a kind of awe in her gaze gave the lie. I left her, and had my foot upon the companion steps, when a thought occurred to me. Going to the door of the captain's berth, I withdrew the wedge, and entered and picked up the pistol that lay upon the deck. It was a heavy single-barrelled concern, but a firearm all the same, and I thrust it into my breast. I perceived no materials for loading it ; but I had what was necessary in that way below ; and now I was possessed, as I did not doubt, of the only two pistols in the ship.

I extinguished the lamp, wedged the door afresh, and responding to Miss Temple's appealing stare with a smile, I went on deck. The night was a clear dusk, with a great plenty of shining stars, over which many small clouds were driving swiftly ; and the wind

still continued to blow strong, though it had
not gained in force since sail had last been
shortened, and the sea was now running
steadily on the bow in regular heaps of dark
waters melting at their heads, so that the
motion of the barque, by being rhythmic, was
comparatively easy. I gained the weather
deck ; and after a peep at the compass and a
glance at the indistinguishable face of the
figure at the wheel, I started off on the tradi-
tionary pendulum walk of the sea-watch, to
and fro, to and fro, from the wheel to the
break of the poop, constantly directing looks
to windward or up aloft, and frequently at
Miss Temple, as she showed, seated as I had
left her, visible to me through the glass of the
skylight. It was out of the question that she
should pace the deck with me throughout that
long watch. The pouring wind came with an
edge of cold damp that made itself felt after
a brief term of exposure to it. Then, again,
it was not to be thought of that the sailors
should find the lady on deck throughout this
night watch, as though we were both in mortal
fear, and kept together to hearten each other.
Now that it had come to there being no head
to the ship, it was of vital importance that Miss

Temple should remain as private as possible, but little seen by the men. I had clear ideas as to the extraordinary situation in which we were placed ; and as I glanced at her through the skylight window, I made up my mind to subdue her to my views, to conquer the insolence of her spirit, even should it come to my having to act in a manner that might be deemed brutal, never to humour her by giving her reasons, but to peremptorily insist in such a fashion as to make her perceive that whilst we were thus together, I was her master, and she must instantly acquiesce in my decisions ; for unless this was to be managed, her temper, her want of tact, her pettish character as that of a person whose nature had been injured by admiration and indulgence, might end in the destruction of us both.

What a midnight watch was that ! I was sick at heart, and miserable with misgiving. My distrust of the carpenter, a feeling that had all along possessed me, was strong even to a conviction that he was equal to the acting of a hellish part, and that being free, and at the head, so to speak, of a gang of men, of whom one only—I mean Wetherly—seemed worthy of confidence, he might be presently hatching some plot of deadly menace to Miss Temple and me. I asked myself what form could such a plot take? I knew not: I could but forebode: I could only keep before me the circumstance of a little ship afloat on a wide sea without captain or mates, full to the hatches with commodities of value, a handsome fabric of herself, virtually in the possession of an irresponsible body of men, into whose keeping she had come through the merest effect of fortune, without the least stroke of . rascality on their part. I say I had only to consider this, and then to think of the character of the crew as it had been represented to me by Captain Braine, to forebode some action on their part that might extinguish my project of reaching Rio—with so much to follow that I durst not give my mind to speculating upon it.

Shocking as had been the suddenness and the unexpectedness of the captain's suicide, the thing sat lightly as a horror upon my imagination, so profoundly agitated was I by the indeterminable fears that had been raised in me by the few words the carpenter had let fall. I could not be sure ; but it seemed to me, by the haze of light which hung about the forecastle hatch, called the forescuttle, and by an occasional stirring of shadows amidst it, as though to the movements of the men below, or to figures coming on deck and descending again, that all hands were awake forward. There should have been nothing to particularly disturb me in this suspicion, for enough lay in the captain's death to account for the men keeping awake and talking; still, the belief that the sailors were conversing in their gloomy little sea parlour, with Lush's growling tongue sulkily active amongst them, greatly increased my uneasiness.

I continued to pace the deck, keeping a close eye upon the ship, with watchful regard also of the compass, for every hour of this sailing was bringing us by so many miles nearer to the South American seaboard. Shortly before two o'clock, on looking through the skylight, I observed Miss Temple lying back upon the cushion of the locker in a sound sleep. Her hat was upon her knees, her cheek was pillowed upon her arm; thus she rested in sideways posture. Whilst I stood looking at her, as at a picture of a beautiful sleeping woman framed in the square of the skylight, and touched with the soft illumination of the oil-lamp swinging hard by her couch, a man struck four bells on the forecastle, and a minute or two later the dark figure of a seaman came along to leeward to relieve the wheel. I waited a little, and then stepped to the binnacle under pretence of inspecting the card.

'Are the watch below up forward?' said I.

'All hands are awake,' he answered, and I recognised him by his voice, though I could not discern his features. He was a young sailor named Forrest, a fellow I had often taken notice of for the elastic suppleness of his body, the peculiar swing of his walk, an amazing agility aloft, and an air of mutinous impudence in his manner of going about any job he might be put to.

'I suppose they have been talking about the captain's death?' said I.

'They've been talking of a many things,' he responded with a sort of chuckle in his voice, as though he had been drinking.

'Is Mr. Lush among them?'

'Oh, ay.'

'Well, keep your luff,' said I; 'she's a couple of points off her course as it is.'

'Her course for where?' said the man.

'For Rio,' I answered.

He made no answer, and I resumed my pacing of the planks.

CHAPTER XXXIII

THE CARPENTER CALLS A COUNCIL

At four o'clock the carpenter came aft to relieve me. He asked me in a short off-hand way how the weather had been; and the wide-awake note in his voice satisfied me that whether or not he had slept during his watch below, he had certainly not now come fresh from his bunk or hammock. When I had answered him, he went abruptly to the compass, and I descended the poop ladder and entered the cuddy.

Miss Temple was still asleep. It was more like some issue of the sorcery of the imagination than the reality to come out of the windy dusk of the night and an association, momentary it might be, with the carpenter, to the spectacle of the slumbering beautiful girl breathing deep and restfully, with the gleam of her white teeth showing through her parted lips, and the lashes of her closed lids resting in a shadow of surprising loveliness upon her colourless cheeks. But rest was imperative to me; there was not another locker to use ; and I would not leave the girl alone. I lightly touched her hand ; she smiled, but slept on ; I touched her again, and she sprang erect with an affrighted air, staring at me with the meaningless gaze of the newly awakened.

'Ah !' she cried with a violent shudder, 'I thought it was the dead captain who touched me ! How cold your hand is.'

'I am going to my berth to seek some rest,' said I ; 'and would not leave you alone here.'

'Oh no !' she exclaimed ; 'I will go with you.'

'You have been sleeping for above two hours,' said I. 'I am very glad. Slumber is strength ; nay, it is life. You have been safe, and you will now tell me that I was in the right in entreating you to remain here.'

'In *commanding* me, you mean,' she answered with a faint smile. 'But how miserable I was alone until I fell asleep—constantly imagining that that door was being cautiously opened' — another strong shudder swept through her while she motioned towards the captain's cabin, holding her face averted.

I unhooked the lantern belonging to my berth, lighted the candle in it, and, taking her by the hand, conducted her to the hatch. When we had entered the steerage, I lifted her hand to my lips in the old-fashioned salute and said : ' Miss Temple, if I appear to *command*, it is with the hope of being useful as a protector to a companion whose claims upon me must needs deepen as we continue together and as the outlook darkens.'

I held open her cabin door for her, gave her my lantern ; and then going to my own berth, groped my way to the bunk, and was speedily in a sound sleep.

It was eight o'clock by my watch when I awoke. I at once sprang out of bed, and, having carefully secreted the pistol I had brought with me from the captain's cabin, I hastily sluiced my face with some salt water, and stepped to Miss Temple's cabin door, on which I knocked. She answered me. I told her that she would find me on deck. ' It is eight o'clock,' I said, ' and my turn to keep watch has come round.' With that I ascended the steps. Wilkins was in the cuddy, as I must needs call the little living-room, though, after the Indiaman's saloon, it seemed a big name to give to so small an interior. I said : ' The lady will be here shortly. Get breakfast ready for us, d'ye hear ? We will eat it on deck, unless there is somebody to keep my lookout whilst I come below for the meal.' He answered, civilly enough, that he would carry it on deck to us on my letting him know when we were ready for it.

I found the carpenter on the poop talking to a couple of seamen ; but on seeing me, the two fellows went forward in a sort of sheepish way. It was a fine morning, lively with flying sunshine, and the seas were running in foaming dark-blue hills, which shouldered the reflection of the sun into incessant flashings of fire as dazzling as the beams darted down by the luminary himself betwixt the edges of the streaming clouds. I sent a swift look round ; there was nothing in sight. The barque was under the same canvas I had left upon her when I went below ; but my first step carrying me to the compass, I perceived that she was making a more southerly course by two points than she had been heading when I left the deck ; and, indeed,

when I directed my eyes aloft for a second
time, I perceived that the yards had been
slightly braced in, and that, in short, Mr
Lush was making a fair wind of what was a
foul one for Rio.   I was greatly startled, but
controlled my face, for the man's eyes were
upon me.

'I presume, Mr. Lush,' said I, crossing
over to him and feigning a certain careless-
ness of behaviour whilst I looked with a manner of indifference past him at the weather
horizon, 'that you are aware the barque is
needlessly off her course, seeing that she'll
easily look up another two or two and a half
points ? '

'A ship's course depends upon where she's
a going,' he answered, running his eyes over my
figure ; 'and nothen's settled yet so far as we're
consarned.'

'Oho !   Is it so, indeed !' said I, after vent-
ing myself in a short whistle.   'What is the
objection to Rio, Mr. Lush ? '

'I'll be calling the crew aft presently,' he
exclaimed ; 'it's a question for all hands, not
for me nor you only, sir.'

'I trust,' said I, my feigned air of careless-
ness vanishing before the real consternation

that was now active in me, 'that the sailors
will not obstruct my earnest desire for the
lady's sake, as well as for my own, to make
for Rio as promptly as possible. Miss Temple
and I have met with some cruel experiences,
and we are as badly off even now, aboard
this smart little barque, as we were in the
wreck from which you rescued us. In God's
name, Mr. Lush, let there be no unreasonable
hindrance to our speedy arrival at a port
whence we may take shipping for home.'

'I have said,' he responded in his sulkiest
manner, 'that it ain't a question for one man
nor for two men, but for all hands.'

I witnessed stubbornness that was to be
easily developed into insolence strong in the
ruffian's face, and bit my lip to silence my
tongue. After a short pause I said: 'I observe that the decks have not been washed
down.'

'No ; that's right. They han't been washed
down.'

'When is the body of the captain to be
buried?'

'He is buried,' he answered; and then
went on, as though perceiving that some explanation was necessary : 'No good in keeping

a human corpse aboard ship. 'Tain't lucky. 'Tain't lucky, even if so be as it's the human corpse of a good man ; but when it comes to the body of the likes of *him*'—— He spat over the rail. ' He was rolled up in canvas and dropped overboard two hours since.'

' A dog's funeral!' said I, betwixt my teeth.

' A dog's funeral's all that the best sailor must expect ; the treatment of a dog when he's alive, and a mongrel's burial when he's dead.'

' Well, I'm here to relieve you,' said I. ' Wilkins will bring my breakfast on deck.'

' All right,' he answered. ' Suppose we call it nine o'clock for the council that's to be held ? '

I turned from him, assenting with a gesture, and walked aft, miserably sick at heart, to receive Miss Temple, who at that moment appeared in the companion way. She instantly perceived by my face that there was something gravely wrong with us, and fixed a look of nervous passionate inquiry upon me. There was no purpose to be served by concealing my fears from her—fears which, shapeless as they might now be, were, I did not question, to be converted presently into bitter convictions. I took her hand and conducted her to the skylight, where we were out of earshot of the helmsman.

'I am afraid,' said I, 'that the death of Captain Braine has thickened the problem of this adventure for us.'

'What has happened?' she demanded.

'When I went below at four o'clock this morning,' I replied, 'the *Lady Blanche* was looking up for the port of Rio as closely as the wind permitted her. Since then, Mr. Lush has taken it upon himself to alter the vessel's course, and we need but another point or two of southing to be sailing straight away down the South Atlantic Ocean.'

'But the ship is *now* being steered for Rio?'

'No.'

'No!' she cried. 'Why do you not order the man to direct her according to your wishes?' And she sent one of her flashing glances at the hairy face of the sailor who grasped the spokes.

'The crew are coming aft presently to settle the question of our destination. I can do nothing. If they have made up their minds to a course, they are not going to suffer me to get in the road of it.'

'But what course? What resolution are they likely to form?' she exclaimed, clasping her hands with a gesture of despair, and gazing forwards with an expression of terror at a group of fellows who stood at the galley door talking.

'I know nothing, and can tell you nothing,' I replied. 'It is to signify another tax upon our patience, and we must wait. Some destination they are bound to hit upon; it will not be Rio, I believe. We shall see. They cannot do without me—that is, I alone am capable of navigating the vessel—and in that may lie our security. But one thing you must help me to achieve, Miss Temple: I mean a behaviour of coolness, good temper, and tact. I believe the devil himself is lodged in the hide of that round-backed brute of a carpenter, and the crew may not be wanting in some of the highest flavoured of his agreeable qualities. Help me, then, to the most inoffensive and patient of attitudes, and say nothing yourself—nay, *look* nothing! for those dark eyes of yours have a hot eloquence of their own, and a man need not hear your rich voice to know what is passing in your mind.'

She forced a calmness upon herself, and spoke in a low voice : ' If the crew insist upon sailing the ship to some distant part, is there nothing that we can do to induce them to transfer us to another vessel, or to run into the land close enough to set us ashore in any town on the coast ? '

' First, let them come to a resolution.'

'This is a shocking situation to be in! Your old energy seems to be leaving you. You give me dreadful news in a lifeless way, and talk spiritlessly of suffering the crew to do as they please.' She said this, still preserving her forced composure ; but there was ire in her gaze and temper and despair in her respiration, in the twitching of the nostril, in the curl of her lip, when she had spoken.

I looked at her steadily, but in silence, weighing down upon her gaze, as it were, with my own until her eyes fell. ' Not spiritless yet,' said I. ' Nor shall I suffer you to make me so, Miss Temple.'

She hung her head, and beat with her fingers upon her knuckles, as though she needed some exercise of that sort to enable

her to suppress her emotions or her tears.
Wilkins came under the skylight to ask if I
was ready for breakfast. I bade him bring it
to us; and he arrived with some coffee and
cold meat and biscuit. I could not induce
the girl to eat. Even when she took a sip of
coffee she scarcely seemed able to swallow it.
Her misery was wretched to see. Sometimes
she would start and send a wild sweeping look
round the horizon; often she would moan.
I tried to put some heart into her; but I could
find little to say, ignorant as I then was of
what the crew meant to do. Most of them
seemed to be in or about the galley. A few
stood in the doorway, and their behaviour
suggested that there were others inside to
whose utterance, whatever form it took, they
listened with attention, sometimes glancing aft
at us. Shortly before nine o'clock I said to
Miss Temple that the crew were coming aft at
that hour, and requested her to go to her own
cabin that she might be out of sight of them.

'Cannot I remain on deck?' she exclaimed.
'My suspense will be a torment. You are
banishing me to an underground cell.'

'You will withdraw to your cabin, if you
please, Miss Temple. We are here dealing

with a crew of men who are now without a head, and whose temper may grow lawless whenever they shall realise that they are their own masters.'

'You will come to me the moment you are at liberty, Mr. Dugdale?'

'Most assuredly.'

I accompanied her to the companion, and watched her as she descended the steps. She halted at the bottom of the ladder to look up at me with eyes of appealing grief. How close she had come to my heart I might not have been able to successfully guess till that moment. I longed to take her in my arms, to entreat her forgiveness for any act or speech of sternness or harshness, to soothe her with all bright and comforting hopes that it was in my power to utter. A step carried her out of my sight, but for some minutes after, the memory of her beautiful appealing eyes dominated all other thoughts, and I could think of nothing but her noble figure, the grief of her colourless high-bred face, the suggestion I found in her attitude of her yearning for my presence and protection—profoundly touching to me who loved her, spite of my knowing that the motive of her longing was to be

---

found in no other sentiment than that of her fear.

Presently the carpenter came out of the galley knocking the ashes out of his pipe, and advanced slowly to the poop, followed by most of the crew, who halted opposite the cuddy front.

'The cabin'll be the place to talk in,' said he; 'there'll be no hearing of one another up here. There's Joe Wetherly'll keep a look-out whilst you and me are below.'

'I am ready,' I answered.

He called to Wetherly, who was standing in the waist, forward of the others. The man touched his cap to me as he ascended the poop ladder, and looked at me meaningly through the minute holes in which his eyes lay deep buried. I entered the cuddy with the carpenter, who turned round as he passed through the door to sing out, 'Step in, lads.' Nine fellows in all followed. Most of them carried a sort of grinning, wondering expression on their faces; but here and there I took note of a determined countenance.

'Mr. Lush,' I exclaimed, 'the ordering of this business is in your hands. I will leave you to settle whatever ceremonies we are to pass through.'

' Mr. Lush'll take the cheer,' said one of the men.

The carpenter at once seated himself in the captain's chair at the after end of the little table. The sailors sat down upon the benches. Lush exclaimed : ' Mr. Dugdale, you sit alongside o' me here. Mates, ease yourselves down, and make room for the gent.'

I took the place he indicated, and waited with as resolved a face as I could screw my features into for what was to follow. There was a pause whilst the carpenter, rolling his eyes over the seamen, seemed to be hunting in his mind for words in which to express himself. The men stared from him to me with an occasional glance round, especially in the direction of the tumbler-rack, at which they would cast thirsty looks. In this brief spell of silence I sought to interpret their intentions from their postures ; but there was little to reassure me in their bearing. There was a kind of defiance in it that instantly made itself felt. They were clad for the most part in shirts and duck or dungaree breeches ;

their breasts were bare, with the sight here
and there of some ink and gunpowder device
straggling amidst the hair ; they leaned upon
their naked muscular arms or sat with them
folded looking at me or the carpenter. There
was no hint of such diffidence as one might
expect to find in forecastle hands occupying
the saloon or cabin of a ship.

'We've been a-tarning over,' began the
carpenter, speaking slowly and viewing me
out of the corners of his eyes, ' the condition
we're put in by the sooicide of Capt'n Braine.
All hands is agreed, saving one, who says that
he dorn't much care how it goes.'

' Who is that one ? ' I asked.

' Joe Wetherly,' he answered.

I waited, but he seemed to require me to
question him.

'You are all agreed, you say, Mr. Lush
—upon what ? '

He coughed, thrust his fingers into his
neckcloth to ease his throat, and then said :
' Well, now, I'll tell ye exactly how it stands.
Wilkins there was next door to the capt'n's
cabin when he told you of that matter of two
hundred thousand pound lying stowed away
in a South Sea island. He comes forward and

tells us all about it.' He paused, then said with a tone of impatience : ' Of course, ye can guess now what we've settled on ? '

' Pray, explain,' said I, understanding but too thoroughly, and feeling the blood forsaking my cheek.

' Why,' said the carpenter with a short laugh, ' what we've resolved on is to sail to that there island and get the money.'

' No good in leaving all that money to lie there for the savages to dig up,' exclaimed one of the men.

' Mr. Lush,' said I, ' I am a stranger in this ship, and have but one desire, and that is, to leave her along with the young lady who was my fellow-passenger aboard the Indiaman. You will of course do what you will with the vessel. The action of the crew can make no part of my business. All that I ask is that you will signal the first vessel we fall in with, let her be heading as she will, and transship us.'

A growling ' No ! ' ran amongst the men. The carpenter echoed it with a blow of his fist upon the table. ' No, sir ! we can't spare you. It'll be *you*, Mr. Dugdale, that'll carry us to that island.'

My consternation was too visible to be missed even by the ignorant eyes which were bent upon me.

'You'll be treated fairly, sir,' said one of the men, with an air and tone of conciliation. 'We've allowed for you being a gent as'll be carried away from the parts he wants to git to. Mr. Lush and us men have talked it well over, and the share of the money ye choose to name is the share you shall have for the time and trouble this bit of navigation'll cost you.'

A murmur of assent followed this speech, several heads nodding so vehemently that their hair danced about their eyes.

'But, men,' I cried, turning upon and addressing them in a body, 'you are surely not going to persuade me that you *believe* in this yarn of the captain?'

'Don't you?' inquired the carpenter with a sarcastic sneer.

'It was the imagination of a madman,' I continued—'a crazy fancy, men! Surely there is no sailor here but knew that the captain was insane. Did not his actions, his talk, his very looks, prove him mad? And what more convincing proof of his insanity could you desire than the last act of his life ?'

Two or three of the fellows grumbled out something, but I did not catch the words. 'Mad, was he?' exclaimed the carpenter in a voice of coarse, morose sarcasm; 'ye didn't think that when you stood out for a share.'

'How do you know,' I cried, 'that I stood out for a share?'

'By God, then,' he roared, 'we know everything! Did ye or did ye not sign an agreement for a share?'

'I did,' I answered, 'but merely to humour the man's madness. I should have left the ship at Rio.'

'There's no use in talking,' he exclaimed, smoothing down his voice a trifle; 'the compact between ye was overheard. Me and the others here was to be got rid of at Rio. Then a crew of Kanakas was to be shipped off the Sandwich Islands. Then, with the gold aboard hidden out of sight, you and him was to ship fresh hands. Mad?' he cried in an indescribably sneering way; 'no, no, that worn't do. Ye didn't think him mad, then, when you made him provide that if the law laid hold of him for a-running away with his ship, you was to be guaranteed free o' peril by what you or him tarmed a hinstrument. Ye didn't think him mad then, and ye don't think him mad now.'

'Wilkins,' I exclaimed to the young fellow who sat at the corner end of the table, 'you overheard that conversation, and your ears were sharp enough to gather in every syllable of it. Were they not sharp enough, my lad, to judge by the tone of my voice that I assented to the madman's humour merely to induce him to make for the near port of Rio, that I and the lady might quickly get away from this vessel?'

The veal-faced fellow stirred uneasily to the many eyes which were turned upon him; but he answered nevertheless with resolution and emphasis: 'You stipulated for tarms, specially for a share, and you spoke as if you was in airnest.'

'Mr. Lush,' I cried, 'I am a gentleman. Believe me, on my honour as one, when I swear to you that I accepted the captain's story as a madman's fabrication, and seemed to agree with him only that I might get away from his ship the sooner.'

'What was the dawcument you signed, sir?' inquired one of the sailors.

'Ah, that's it,' cried another; 'let's see the hinstrument, as Mr. Lush tarms it.'

I had them both in my pocket-book, intending to preserve them as curiosities and as illustrations of my adventure with Miss Temple. I could not refuse to produce them, nor would I stoop to a falsehood; but I was sensible as I drew out the pocket-book, intently watched by the seamen, that the mere circumstance of my carrying the papers about with me as though I deemed them too precious to be laid aside in a drawer, told heavily against the assurance I had made to the men. The carpenter picked the documents up.

'Who can read here?' said he, looking round. There was no reply. 'Will you recite 'em, sir?' he continued, turning his surly eyes upon me.

'There's Joe as can read,' broke in a voice.

'Ay, call Joe,' exclaimed another man.

This signified that I was not to be trusted. They might suppose I would invent instead of reading, and there was no man present able to spell a word to disprove what I chose to deliver. The lee lid of the skylight lay open. The carpenter roared through it for Joe Wetherly, who promptly stepped below.

'What is it?' he asked, looking round upon his mates.

'Here, Joe,' said the carpenter, 'you're the one scholard aboard us. Tarn to, will 'ee, and let's hear what's wrote down upon these papers.'

The man glanced at me with an expression of sympathy and bashfulness. 'I hope there's nothen private and agin your wish in this, sir?' he exclaimed. 'I'm for standin' neutral in this here job.'

'Pray read,' said I.

He did so, backing and filling in his postures in true sailor fashion as he struggled through the writing, reciting the words slowly, with considerable pauses between, which furnished his hearers with time to digest what he delivered. He then put the papers down, but with an air of astonishment, as I noticed with grief and anxiety, as if having been before incredulous of the captain's story, he was beginning to regard it as a fact now in the face of such documentary evidence as he had read.

'All right, Joe; thank ye,' said the car-

penter gruffly; 'you can go on deck agin.'
The man went up the ladder slowly, as though
lost in thought. 'Lads,' exclaimed Lush,
'ye'll agree with me there's no need for further
arguefication after what ye've just heard.'

'The money's right enough, and we'll git
it,' said one of the men.

'Where's the chart of the island as Wilkins
said the captain talked about?' inquired the
limber bold-faced young seaman with whom I
had spoken at the wheel when I found the
barque off her course.

All eyes were at once turned upon me.
'You'll find it in the drawer of the table of
the captain's cabin,' said I.

The fellow coolly entered the berth, and
presently returned with a handful of papers.
'Which 'll it be, sir?' he exclaimed, placing
them before me. I picked up the parchment
chart, and gave it to the carpenter, who spread
it out before him, and instantly all the men
came round to his chair, and stood in a heap
of shouldering figures mowing and mopping
over his shoulders to catch a view, tossing the
hair with jerks of their heads out of their
eyes, and breathing hard with excitement.

'I suppose you're capable of explaining

the meaning of these here marks?' exclaimed the carpenter, pressing a shovel-shaped thumb upon the outline of the island.

'You shall have the yarn as the captain gave it me,' said I, speaking with a throat dry with mortification and sickness at heart; for it was only too certain now that my agreements with the captain coupled with this chart had hardened the men's conviction into an immovable resolution. They listened with breathless interest as I told them that the barb of the arrow indicated the situation of the buried money; that the treasure lay hidden so many paces away from the wash of the water of the lagoon; that the blot in the centre of the bight was meant to express a coral pillar that served as a mark to obtain the bearings of the gold by; and so on. I see their feverish eyes as I write coming and going from my face to the chart, and the various expressions of exultation, eager determination, amazement, and delight on the mob of countenances over the carpenter's shoulders.

'You now have what the captain explained to me,' said I; 'but he was a madman, men; and I take God to witness that though this island may be real, the money is the coinage of a diseased mind.'

'Yet ye would not stir till you had made him agree to give you a share,' said the carpenter. 'Boys, back to your places whilst I delivers the resolution we have all of us made up our minds to.'

The sailors hurriedly resumed their seats. The carpenter gazed slowly round, then addressed me with his eyes in the corner of their sockets whilst his face pointed straight down the table.

'We're here without a capt'n,' he began, 'and though this barque ain't ourn, we mean to use her. We don't intend no act of piracy. When we've got the gold, we'll deliver up the ship and her cargo, which we shan't meddle with. We're all of us working men, and the money in that there island fairly distributed 'll make all hands of us independent for life. There's no more involved than the job of fetching it, and that's to be easily managed.' The men nodded emphatically. 'You're a navigator, Mr. Dugdale, and we can't do without ye. There's no good in talking of shipping another man in your place, because, d' ye see, that 'ud oblige us either to com-

municate with a passing vessel or to put into
some port, neither of which is to be henter-
tained, seeing the nature of the secret which
is ourn, and which we mean to keep ourn.
We're agreeable to con-sider any tarms ye
may think proper to propose. As has bin
said, the share ye name is the share ye'll
have. Ye shall be capt'n, and treated as
capt'n. You and the lady shall live in this
here part of the ship without mollystation, as
the saying is; and ye'll find us a perlite and
willing crew, who'll stick to our side of the
compact as *you* stick to yourn. The money
ye'll get by this job, gent as ye are, will re-
pay both you and the lady for loss o' time and
for work done. This here barque knows how
to sail, and neither me nor you'll spare her;
for we're now in a hurry and this voyage can't
end too quickly to please us all. Them's our
tarms, which ye can put into writing if you
please, and we'll write our marks agin it.
There must be no communicating with ships;
and *ye've got to be honest!*' He said this with
a sudden frown, looking full at me. 'Is that
your mind, men?'

There was a hurricane response of 'Ay,
ay! That's right; that's right.'

'Give me a little while to consider,' said I, observing that the carpenter had come to an end.

'By when will we have your answer?' he demanded.

'By noon.'

'Agreed,' he exclaimed. 'Here's your two documents. I'll take charge of this here chart.'

A few minutes later I was alone.

CHAPTER XXXIV

I ASSENT

I SAT as the sailors had left me at that table, lost in thought, bending all the energies of my mind to full realisation of my situation, that my judgment might soundly advise me. I daresay I remained thus for above twenty minutes as motionless as ever was the dead figure that we had met with in the deck-house of the wreck. Then slowly rising, I went to one of the cabin windows and stood mechanically staring at the piebald sky that would come with a sweep, as the vessel rolled to windward, to the throbbing line of the frothing horizon ; and thus I continued, still thinking, weighing one consideration and then another, forming resolutions which the next effort of thought rendered helplessly idle, until I had arrived at a determination ; when, starting from my deep and painful reverie, I descended into the steerage and knocked on

Miss Temple's cabin door. She immediately opened it.

'At last!' she cried. 'Oh, Mr. Dugdale, what have you to tell me now?'

'Let us go to the cabin,' I answered; 'we shall be alone there. The gloom of these quarters is horribly depressing.'

My manner caused her to regard me for a moment or two with a feverish eagerness of scrutiny; she then mounted the steps, and I followed her.

'I wish I had news to give that might comfort you,' said I, seating myself at her side. 'The men left me half an hour ago. I have been thinking my hardest since, and will tell you now how matters stand, and how I believe I must act.'

She breathed quickly, but said nothing. Her eyes devoured me, so passionate was her curiosity and fear.

'The captain's conversation with me,' I began, 'was, as you know, overheard by the rogue Wilkins, who waits upon us. He must have hearkened thirstily; not a syllable did he lose, and every sentence he carried forward to the crew. They are fully convinced of the truth of the crazy story; they are firmly per-

suaded that there are some two hundred
thousand pounds' worth of golden coin buried
in that South Sea island ; they were also
made aware by that scoundrel listener that I
had insisted upon having an agreement signed
and witnessed ; which of course confirmed
them in their opinion that I myself believe in
the captain's story up to the hilt.   Their demand, then, is, that I should navigate the ship
to the island, that they may dig up the money
hidden in it.'

She listened with silent horror.

'They laugh at my assurance that the
captain was mad,' I went on, 'and they see
nothing in his suicide to cause them to doubt
that his story is absolutely true.'

'And what did you tell them?'

'That I must have time to think, and will
give them an answer by noon.'

'What *do* you think?' she demanded,
searching my gaze with her proud eyes.

'I see nothing for it but to undertake to
sail the ship to the South Pacific.'

'Are you mad?' she almost shrieked. 'To
the South Pacific ! Did you not say to them
that you will insist upon their stopping the

first ship that passes, and putting you and me
on board of her?'

'They are not to be reasoned with,' I
answered gently; 'the dream of this gold has
raised an appetite in them that might easily
convert them into wild beasts, if I refuse to
help them to satisfy their hunger. They will
not suffer communication with any passing
vessel; they will not permit me to make for
any port. Their proposal is that I shall be captain, and have, with you, the exclusive use of
this end of the ship, and they promise me handsome usage. But underlying the terms they
desire me to agree to is a menace that I should
be blind not to see. I must do what they want,
or what that villain Lush has contrived that
they shall want, or God alone knows what the
issue may be for you as well as for myself.'

She sat viewing me like one paralysed.

'My intention,' I went on, 'is to inform
the carpenter at noon that I assent to the
wishes of the crew.'

She was about to speak; I held up my
hand.

'I entreat you to let me have my way.
Do not reason. You can offer no remedy for
this situation saving that of haughty demand,

which, unless you can back it, as a theory of
escape, by a gang of men capable of pistolling
the fellows forward, will be of no more use to
you or to me than a feather to a drowning
man.   My resolution is, to consent to navigate
this vessel to that South Sea island.   The
island may be an imaginary one; the crew's
disappointment may force us into a hunt;
they will then certainly believe that the captain's story was the fancy of a madman, and
will ask me to carry them to some near port.
This will be the issue of the adventure, supposing it is all smooth sailing till then.   But
what may happen meanwhile ?   A storm
to cripple us, and force us to seek assistance ?
The sea abounds in the unexpected.   We must
wait upon fortune.   Nothing shall tempt me
to endeavour to force her hand by any sort of
demeanour that is not one of tact, good temper, and secret, iron-hard resolution to snatch
at the first chance that may come along.
Why, is not such a policy as this your due,
Miss Temple?   Compared to what *might*
happen if I did not deal with these men as a
combustible not on any account whatever to
be approached with matter that could give
fire to them, this existence, this unendurable

existence which we are now passing through
might be looked back upon as a veritable
paradise. I am one to twelve, and you have
no protector but me. Think of it! Bear with
my judgment then ; help me by striving to
witness wisdom in my determination ; and
above all keep up your heart, which is an
Englishwoman's, whose pulse should grow
stronger as the road grows darker.'

She had put her hands to her face, and so
sat listening to me, slightly rocking herself.
Presently she looked up.

'I wish I had the spirit you ask me to
show,' she said in a low voice. 'You may have
resolved rightly—but this long alienation from
home—the misery of this existence—the peril
we are in, which every day, which every hour,
seems to increase—oh, it is hard to bear! I
will endeavour to school myself. I will strive
to see with your eyes'—she broke off with a
sob.

'All will come right,' I exclaimed ; 'it is
entirely a question of waiting. Have you
patience? Yes—and your patience will keep
you hopeful. Trust to me and to my judgment.'

I took her hand in both mine and pressed

it. She did not offer to withdraw it. Indeed, it seemed as though she found comfort in the clasp; her hard expression of consternation softened, and her fine eyes took the same air of appeal I had noticed in them when she went below to her cabin.

'There is yet the chance,' I said, 'of my being able to persuade the crew to transfer you to a passing ship. I might indeed,' I went on, warming up to the fancy, 'insist upon this as a part of my agreement with them.'

She slightly shook her head and her glance fell.

'How long will it take us to reach this island?' she asked, keeping her gaze bent down.

'Ten or twelve weeks, perhaps.'

She bit her lip to enable her to speak steadily, and said: 'Supposing there is no gold, what will be done?'

'I cannot tell,' I answered; 'we may be quite certain that there is no gold. It yet remains to be seen whether even the poor wretch's island is real.'

'If there should be no island, Mr. Dugdale?'

' Well, as I just now said, the men will at
first suppose me wrong in my navigation, and
oblige me to keep on hunting about for a bit.
But such a quest will not take long to tire
them, and they will probably ask me to carry
them on to the coast.'

' To what part?'

' Valparaiso, probably. That will be a
near port in those seas.'

' At that rate,' she exclaimed with an
expression of impatience and dismay, ' we
shall be sailing about for five or six months
without the least opportunity of my getting
on shore, of my returning home, of my being
able to obtain a change of dress.'

' Providing nothing happens. And even
assuming that you are forced to see this adventure out to the bitter end, the worst that
befalls you is a disagreeably long divorce
from your home, together with such discom-
forts as you should laugh at when you think
of them side by side with the tragedy that
this ramble is easily to be worked into.'

However, spite of her little effort to look
the difficulty in the face, she seemed stunned.
She would start sometimes whilst I talked to
her, and send a wild sweeping look round the

cabin, as though she could not realise her situation and sought to persuade herself that she was in a dream. I was grieved for her beyond words, yet I would not exhibit too much sympathy either, lest I should unduly accentuate the significance of our condition, and make her suppose that I believed it darker and more perilous than it really was. She had been buoyed up with a hope of escaping into another ship, or of shortly landing at Rio, and sailing home from there ; and the disappointment coming on top of the perception that our adventure, harsh and soul-subduing as it had already been in some particulars, was only in reality just beginning, seemed to break her down. I did my utmost to make light of the business : said that but for my anxiety for her, I should enter upon the affair with positive relish, accepting it as a wild romance of the sea, which could seldom happen to a man in his life, and which he ought to live through and see out, if only for the sake of the memory of a stirring picturesque passage that at the longest would yet be brief.

'As to wearing-apparel,' I said, ' there are needles and thread forward, and I don't

doubt that when you are put to it you will
be able to manage. And then, suppose this
story of the captain's should prove true! suppose we should actually find buried in the
spot he indicated a mass of gold which, when
equally divided amongst us, would yield every
man several thousands of pounds!'

She searched my face with her glowing eyes. 'You do not believe this?' she
cried.

'Certainly I do not,' I answered. 'I am
only supposing.' .

'I wish I could read your heart; I wish
I could be sure that your determination to
assent to the men's wishes is not owing to
sympathy with their own ideas.'

I burst into a loud laugh. 'Of how
many sins do you think me capable?' I
exclaimed. 'How many enormous follies am
I equal to? I believe you already secretly
regard me as a pirate. Oh, Miss Temple, no
man could ever feel ill-tempered in conversing with you, say what you will. But you
are a little trying, though, now and again.
Why do you wish to read my heart? You
might discover sentiments which would render
me detestable to you.'

'I do not understand you,' she exclaimed, looking somewhat frightened.

'Admiration for you, in a person whom you dislike, would make you abhor him.'

'Mr. Dugdale, is this a time for such feeble small-talk as would scarcely be endurable amidst safety and comfort? I should not be so utterly unhappy as I am if I felt that my mother knew where I was, that she was conscious of all that has happened to me, and that we should meet again.'

'It will all come right,' said I, looking at my watch. 'I must make ready now for taking sights, and letting the carpenter know the determination I have arrived at. Back me, Miss Temple, in my efforts by the utmost exertion of your tact. And now, come on deck with me, will you? There is life in the fresh and frothing scene outside, and you will find courage in the mere sight of the wide horizon, with thoughts of what lies behind it, and how time will work all things to your wishes.'

I entered the captain's cabin to fetch a sextant, and then, with Miss Temple, went on deck. Lush was marching up and down the weather side of the poop. The sailors were

sprawling about forward in whatever shadow-
ings of the canvas they could find, most of
them smoking, their faces red as powder-flags
with the heat. Hot it was, with the sun
shining nearly over our mastheads, with a
sting like to some fierce bite in every flashing
launch of his radiance betwixt the wool-white
clouds blowing transversely athwart his path,
spite of the strong sweep of the wind as it
came splitting in long whistlings upon our
rigging from a little forward of the beam, the
rush of it feeling almost damp to the flesh to
the view of the foaming waters melting into
yeast out of the long blue lines of the Atlantic
surge. The barque, making a fair breeze of
it, was storming through the seas in noble
style, shouldering off vast masses of throbbing
white from her weather bow with a wake
twisting away astern of her of twice her beam
in width, a broad path of glittering, leaping,
blowing crystals and foam-flakes and creaming
eddies rising and falling for a mile astern into
the windy blue there, full of fire and snow
as it looked with the spume of breaking
waves and the splendour of the darting sun-
light.

The carpenter came to a stand when I

arrived. I went up to him at once, Miss
Temple at my side.

'I have thought the matter over,' I said,
'and accept the men's terms.'

'Glad to hear it,' he answered, with a slow
smile breaking sulkily through his surly countenance. 'If you care about a written hunder-
taking '——

'No,' I interrupted contemptuously ; 'my
agreement is based on yours. If you do not
hold piously to every article of it, I drop my
part.'

He viewed me with his head slightly on
one side, but without any appearance of resentment at my peremptory tone. Coarse and
unlettered as the fellow was, he had discern-
ment enough to witness what he would regard
as sincerity of purpose in my very outspoken-
ness.

'All you've got to do,' said he, 'is to carry
us to that there island. You do your bit, and
you'll have no occasion to grumble at us for
not doing ourn. But—you'll *do* it. You
onderstand me, Mr. Dugdale ? So long as
you're honest, you'll find *us* honest.'

The ugly significance he imparted to these
words by the look that accompanied them, I

could not hope to express. Miss Temple, whose hand was on my arm, shrank at my side. It pleased me that she should have witnessed that look and heard the words, for they would go further to persuade her that the only road to choose in this matter was the one I had taken, than any amount of reasoning on my part.

'Your threats are perfectly indifferent to me,' I exclaimed, eyeing him coolly and fixedly. 'I believe I know your character, and don't question your capacity to act up again to the part your captain told me you had already played.'

'What was that?' he growled, but with no other change of face than such as temper might produce. I seemed to find even in this little thing that the captain had told me a lie when he charged the fellow with murder, and my mind felt easier on a sudden as to a conviction of the truth of a matter less dark than I had dared believe.

'That is my business,' I responded, preserving my cool almost contemptuous manner. 'You need be at no pains to threaten me. You'll achieve nothing by your forecastle menaces. I have been a sailor in my time

and quite know what you and such as you
are. If you or any of your mates disappoint
me in a single particular of the understanding
between us, I will throw this sextant,' said I,
flourishing it under his nose, ' overboard, and
you may grope your way round the Horn as
best you can.   That agreement is this:' I
elevated my forefinger. ' First we are to have
the exclusive use of this end of the ship ; you
alone coming aft to stand your watch.' He
nodded. I erected another finger. 'Next:
the captain's cabin and the one adjoining are
to be occupied by this lady and myself.' He
nodded again. I raised a third finger, thrusting it close to his face. ' Next : Wilkins con-
tinues to wait upon us as heretofore ; we are
to be fed with care and punctuality ; it is distinctly to be understood—and this *you* will
see to—that no liquor aboard is broached
outside a tot or two per man per day ; for,'
said I, speaking with the most emphatic
deliberateness I could contrive, ' if there
should be a single exhibition of drunkenness
amongst the crew, I shall pitch this sextant
overboard.'

' I've got nothen to say agin that,' he exclaimed, speaking with something of sullen

respect, as though impressed by my energy and language.

'Next,' I proceeded, 'I am to be captain, and what I say must be law, and what I do must be done.'

'Saving this,' said he, elevating two square fingers in imitation of my gesture : 'Fust, you ain't going to order us to speak a ship, and next you ain't going to get us to obey ye if you should take it into your head to steer for a port.'

'No,' I replied, 'that is a part of my agreement. Yet there is this to be said : it is mere idle cruelty to carry this young lady away round Cape Horn into the Pacific. She is without any other wearing apparel than what you see ; she is destitute of almost every convenience ; her mother is in bad health, and she wishes to return as speedily as possible, that no news about us may reach England that is not perfectly true. The crew, therefore, will not object to speak a ship that we may transfer this lady to her.'

'No !' he roared.

'Her going will render me easy in my mind as to her safety,' I continued, 'and I shall be able to serve you the better by knowing that she is on her way home.'

'No!' he roared again; 'she's quite safe aboard us. There must be no speaking with ships. 'Sides,' he added, falling back a step with a round flourish of his arm, 'the lady knows all about the gold and where it is and how it's to be come at.'

'I can keep a secret, Mr. Lush,' she exclaimed.

'No,' he repeated with a stamp of his foot; 'sorry for it, lady, but here ye are, and here ye must stop. I know what the crew 'ud say. I'm but expressing of their minds. Here ye stop, lady. Mr. Dugdale, that was a part of the bargain, as we onderstood it this marning. Besides, lady,' he added with an indescribable leer, 'ye wouldn't care to be separated from him *now*, would 'ee?'

She moved so as to bring him between me and her.

'That will do, Mr. Lush,' said I. 'I am acquainted with your wishes, and you know now my resolution;' and so saying, I walked to a part of the deck where I could command the sun, and went to work with my sextant, talking to Miss Temple in a low voice as I ogled the luminary.

'You see now how it is? If I refused my assent to the crew's wishes, they might have sent me adrift in a boat—alone,' I added significantly.

'He is a most dreadful creature. You spoke to him bravely. But is that manner what you call tact?'

'Yes. The man must not imagine that I am afraid of him. I would that I could choke him with his own threats.'

'I believe he would not shrink from murdering both of us.'

'They have made up their minds to sail to the island, and they mean that I shall carry them there. That resolve was strong in them when they entered the cabin. If I had refused—— But no matter! It may yet come to my being able to induce them to speak a ship.'

She made no response. There was a short silence between us.

'Make eight bells!' I shouted, and the chimes floated sharp upon the rushing wind as I walked aft to the companion, Miss Temple always at my side.

I went straight to the captain's cabin, and there worked out my observation, and fixed the correct position of the barque on the chart. The course she was steering happened to be the true direction she needed to take, and there was nothing to mend in that way. Miss Temple came to the table and watched me as I made my calculations. When I had come to an end, I asked her to remain where she was, and returned with the chart on deck. I beckoned to the carpenter, who was standing at the break of the poop, as though waiting for me to arrive that he might go forward to his dinner.

'Here's our situation to-day,' I exclaimed pointing to the chart—it was a tract-chart of the world—' and here's Cape Horn. Our course then is as we're steering.'

He stared at the chart with the blind and stupid look of a man who cannot read, and after a bit said : ' Let's see : here's south, and here's west, ain't it ? And here's Cape Horn, as you say. Ay, our course is about right for it, I allow.'

Whilst I rolled the chart up, I exclaimed : ' It is inconvenient to be without a stand-by for a third relief. You and I both want to dine at once, and there is nobody to keep a lookout in the place of one of us. The man who had charge this morning whilst we were below appeared to be a very respectable steady sailor. Suppose now, calling me captain, and you chief officer, we appoint him, with the sanction of the crew of course, second mate.'

'I dunno as I should do that,' he answered; 'best not have too many masters aboard. *I'm* no chief officer, and there'll be no convartin' of Joe Wetherly into a second mate. We're all jest *men*. But I tell 'ee what; if the crew's willing, Joe might be selected to relieve you or me whensoever it comes about as the pair of us wants to be below at the same time, as now.'

'Very well,' I exclaimed, in the sort of peremptory yet half-careless way which I had made up my mind to employ when speaking to this man; 'work it out in your own fashion. You can send him aft to relieve me when he's done dinner. I shall feel obliged by your seeing that Wilkins turns to and prepares the table for us at once.'

I was about to leave him, when he exclaimed: 'One question, Mr. Dugdale. Nothen was said between us men and you as to the share ye expect.'

'Never mind about that now,' I answered.

'The agreement betwixt you and the captain was for a third, I think,' said he ; ' you won't expect that, now there's a dozen of us in the consarn ? '

'Oh no, oh no ! Send Joe Wetherly aft as soon as he's done.'

'It's onderstood,' said he, ' that the lady won't take no share?'

'Yes, you may understand that,' I exclaimed. 'As for my portion,' I continued, anxious to get rid of him, ' give me what you think I shall have fairly earned, and you'll satisfy me.'

'Right!' he exclaimed with alacrity, seeking clumsily to conceal an emotion of sulky exultation. 'Just another word, Mr. Dugdale. What sort of character might that ha' been which the captain gave me?'

'Oh, damn it! go and send Joe Wetherly aft,' I cried, feigning a fit of temper ; and I marched away to the binnacle, leaving him to trudge forward.

A few minutes later, on looking through the skylight, I perceived Wilkins preparing the table. Presently, Wetherly arrived on the poop. I went forward to meet him, that I might be out of ear-shot of the fellow at the wheel, and at once said : 'Wetherly, how is it with you in this truly infernal business?'

'Truly infarnal it is, sir,' he instantly replied ; 'but you've got the most raw-headed lot of men to deal with that ever slung hammocks in a ship's forecastle. After they went forward last night, they fell a-debating, all hands of them, and settled for this ship to fetch away that there gold, you commanding. I was agin it till I see how hot they talked, and then I thinks says I to myself, what do it sinnify? Whether I'm bound away to the Isle o' France or to a loonatic's island in the South Pacific, is all the same. If there's money there, so much the better. If there ain't, it can't be helped. One agin ten's not going to do much aboard a ship ; so, when I was asked for an opinion, I just says, I'm neutral, lads. Do as ye like. I'll be with ye ; but never none of ye go and ask if I'm *of* ye.'

'You don't surely believe in Captain Braine's crazy fancy?'

'Well, I own, Mr. Dugdale, that that

there agreement 'twixt you and him a bit
nonplushed me this mornin' after I had read
it out.   It did look oncommonly like as
though you yourself genu-inely believed in
the yarn.'

He viewed me critically, though respectfully, as he spoke, with his mere pins'-heads of
eyes.

'Oh, man, I agreed—I pretended to fully
credit—wholly with the idea of coaxing the
madman to Rio, where the lady and myself
would have left the barque.   Can't you see
that, Wetherly ? '

' Why, yes,' he answered quickly, though
speaking, nevertheless, as though his mind
was not quite made up.   'It's a bad job for
you and the lady, sir.   The men are terribly
in airnest.   They'll allow no speaking with
ships, for fear of your blowing the gaff, as the
saying goes.   I may tell you you've acted
wisely in falling in with their wishes.   I may
be more open by and by.   I'm with you
and the lady, sir ; but I've got to be very careful.'

' I thank you sincerely.'

I saw him restlessly glance aft at the helmsman, and took the hint. His goodwill was of the utmost importance to me, and it would not do to imperil my relations with him by any sort of behaviour that might excite the suspicions of the crew as to our intimacy.

CHAPTER XXXV

I AM arrived now at a passage of this singular
adventure that will admit only of brief indications of certain features of it. To write down
all the incidents of the time which followed
could but run me into several volumes of very
insipid matter. I own that when I look back
upon this experience, it offers itself as something so amazing, something so beside the
most astonishing romantic incidents of sea-life
which my memory carries, that, though I was
the chief actor in it, I often at this hour find
myself pausing as in doubt of the actuality of
the events I have related and have yet to
narrate.

Sometimes I wonder whether I might not
have brought this kidnapping business—for
thus it may fairly be called so far as Miss
Temple and I were concerned—to a speedy
end by peremptory refusal to navigate the

ship to Captain Braine's island. But I have only to close my eyes and recall the faces and recollect the behaviour of the men who formed that barque's crew, to know better; I have only to repeople that now timeworn canvas with the countenances of those seamen, to witness afresh the looks and bearing of the carpenter, to recollect my defencelessness, the helplessness of my companion, whose life and whose more than life were absolutely dependent upon my judgment; to think of the wild greed raised in the men by their dream of thousands, their resolution to get the money, the sense of lawlessness that would increase upon them with the growing perception of their irresponsibility as a crew deprived of their officers by no crime of their own : I have only to recall all this along with my own thoughts and fears and bitter nerve-sapping anxieties, to understand that the course I adopted was the only practicable one open to me, and that what I did no other man situated as I then was but must have also done. But enough of this.

That afternoon, when the carpenter relieved me at four o'clock, I went below and superintended the preparation of the two cabins at the extremity of the cuddy for our reception. The berth adjoining the captain's was a fresh, bright, airy little apartment, and every convenience that Braine's cabin yielded was put into it for Miss Temple's use. This change of apartment seemed to tranquillise her a bit. Such was her dislike and fear of our steerage quarters, that I believe she would have thought the deck-house of the wreck endurable compared to them. Instead of a little 'tweendeck shrouded in gloom and lumbered with cargo, we had the whole breezy, sun-lit cuddy before us when we opened our doors. The berths were also well lighted, with something of taste in their equipment of panel, bulkhead mouldings, and the like. I was very careful to bring up Mr. Chicken's pistol and ammunition, and when I was alone with Miss Temple, I said : ' You are not afraid to handle a firearm, I think ? '

' Oh dear, no.'

' You shot very well, I remember, with Mr. Colledge at a bottle. Who hit the bottle ?'

' I did.'

' So I might have thought by your manner of aiming at it. Your figure showed nobly, Miss Temple, in your posture as markswoman. I remember the sparkle of your eyes as you glanced along the barrel. I should not have cared to be hated by you and in front of you at that moment.'

'I wish I had the courage you feign I have,' said she.

'Well,' I exclaimed, pulling the captain's pistol out of my breast, 'here is a friend that will do more than bark for you, if you should find yourself in want of such help as it can give. I have a double-barrelled concern of a like build in the next room, so that between us we are able to muster three muzzles; artillery enough to fit us to stand a siege, I can assure you, with the ammunition we possess.'

She took the clumsy weapon in her small delicate white hand and toyed with it, levelling and examining it, and so forth. I bade her mind, as it was loaded. She smiled, and going to her bunk, hid the pistol between the mattress and the bulkhead.

'I shall certainly feel easier for having it,' said she. 'You will not always now be next door, Mr. Dugdale. You will be for four hours at a time on deck, when you keep your watch.'

'Ay,' said I; 'but there is a skylight;

and I'll take care that the cabin lamp be kept burning ; and I have a keen ear, too, that when I am away from you will not be blunted by my thoughts always being here.'

My own cabin I found comfortable enough. I was not so choice as to be above using what I found in it. The unhappy captain had left behind him sufficient clothes to provide me with several changes : and a couple of his coats fitted me very well—being made, I suppose, to allow for a sailor's underclothing in cold weather—though I was much broader in the shoulders than he had been. I overhauled his papers, but found nothing of interest. What I met with I carefully put away in a drawer along with some money, and one or two objects of some small value, for I remembered that the unfortunate creature had left a widow behind him, who might be thankful for his poor effects, should the little ship ever live to carry his goods and his tragic story to a civilised place.

Wilkins waited upon us with punctuality and civility. He would ask me what I wished for breakfast and dinner and supper, bringing little suggestions from the cook as to sea-pies and ship-board hashes and currant dumplings and other heavy dishes, for the due digestion of which a man needs to have bowels of brass and the triple rows of the shark's fangs. Indeed, the *Lady Blanche's* larder was a poor one, and the genius of the first cook in the world must have come to a halt in the face of such a Mother Hubbard of a cupboard. Aft, there was little more to eat than the forecastle stores: salt beef and salt pork, peas, currants for duff days, biscuit, coffee and tea, and a few other items. However, the dead captain had laid in a good stock of bottled beer. There were also a few gallons of brandy and gin, both of them a very good spirit ; and the forecastle stores, supplemented by cheese and hams and some tins of preserved stuff bearing the name of soup and bouilli—pronounced by sailors soup and bully, or soap and bullion—supplied us with dishes enough to enable us to support life and even health, helped out as they were by occasional little relishes from the cook, feeble attempts indeed, and briny to a degree, yet in their way welcome to people who were as good as beggars in food, and without choice.

Lush faithfully kept to his end of the ship. He never offered to enter the cabin except to my invitation, when perhaps I

would have something in navigation to tell
him about. He seemed anxious to keep us at
a distance, and picked up the ship's routine,
when his watch came round, as I let it fall,
with an air of morose reserve. I made
several efforts with an assumption of cheerfulness and heartiness of manner to break
through his sullenness, with the dream of
finding something like a human being of sensi-
bilities behind it, whom I should be able to
influence into getting the crew to consent to
speak a passing ship, that Miss Temple might
be transferred to her; but he was like a
hedgehog; his quills regularly rose to my
least approach. He would watch me with a
sulky, cursing expression in his eye, or view
me with a sour, askant regard, and to my
civillest speech respond in some ragged,
scurvy sentence.

But I did not play an obliging part with
him very long. Having come to the conclusion that he was a ruffian of immovable
qualities, I recurred to my earlier behaviour,
addressed him only to give him instructions
in a peremptory manner, or to point out the
ship's place on the chart; so, as you will suppose, very little passed between us; yet my

putting on the airs of a captain and treating him as the mere forecastle hand which he claimed to be, influenced his bearing, and rendered him even respectful.

Nevertheless, I knew that he and his mates never had their eyes off me, so to speak; that, having learnt the course to Cape Horn was so-and-so, the compass was watched with restless assiduity, every man as he was relieved at the wheel reporting the direction of the ship's head to his companions forward, and how she had been steering during his trick; that my behaviour on deck was critically followed by eyes in the fore-part of the ship; that I could never give an order to trim sail during my watch but that it was duly reported to Lush, and weighed and considered by the crew in the frequent councils they held in the caboose. All this I was secretly informed of by Wetherly.

Yet I had nothing to complain of in the behaviour of the men. They sprang to my bidding, and their 'Ay, ay, sirs,' and responses to my orders had as lively and hearty a ring as anyone could hope to hear in the mouth of a crew. They sang out briskly when they pulled and hauled, with enjoyment of the sound of their own voices, and a marked willingness in their demeanour to contribute their utmost to the navigation of the vessel. This, indeed, was to be expected. It was rather a Jack's jaunt now with them, than a voyage; they were sailing, as they believed, to an island full of gold; their fortunes were assured; they gazed into a future radiant with visions of dancing, drinking, marine jinks of all sorts; they knew that the fulfilment of their fine lookout must depend upon their willingness to work the ship now, so that everything they did they did without a growl; without the least hint of the mutinous disposition that would have shown strong and deadly in them, had their wishes been delayed or obstructed.

But outside the actual, essential routine of the ship, nothing was done. The decks were washed down at very long intervals only; there was no sail-making or repairing; the spunyarn winch was mute; the chafing gear was left to rot off as it would; the carpenter indeed saw to the rigging, took care that everything should be sound, for neither he nor his mates had a mind to lose a mast. But there was very little of sweeping or polishing, of swabbing or cleaning.

The rum was kept down in the steerage; every day Wilkins drew as much as sufficed to furnish the men with two glasses apiece. After drawing the stuff, he regularly presented himself with it to Lush or me, according as the one or the other of us was on deck, that it might be seen he had drawn the allowance only. The men seemed fully satisfied. There was never any demand for more grog than what was given to them, and I do not recall a single instance of intoxication; which I attributed to my determined and oft-repeated declaration that should there be any exhibition of drunkenness on board the barque, I would abandon my undertaking, and leave the carpenter to navigate her. Dread of the consequences of drink amongst a mob of such ungoverned men as those fellows, rendered me extraordinarily impressive and emphatic in this threat: and I knew that the carpenter was convinced in his own mind that I would prove as good as my word. Indeed, I had only to look at Miss Temple to shrink from the mere thought of drunkenness amongst the sailors. All other risks that might attend a drinking bout forward were as naught compared to the peril *she* would stand in. The

least insult offered her I should resent with
the muzzle of my pistol ; and if it ever came
to *that*, then God alone could foresee the
character of the tragedy that must follow.

But, as I have said, they showed themselves satisfied with their two glasses a day.
The sense of festivity never carried them
further than an occasional dance on the forecastle head of a fine dog watch, when they
would diversify their caper-cutting with
songs and yarns—all as harmless as child's
play, so unsuggestive of the errand that we
were upon, so dumb as indications of the
smouldering fires which were to be blown
into a blaze by want of judgment on my part,
that any one viewing us from the deck of a
ship close at hand would have supposed the
Lady Blanche the very peacefullest of traders,
worked by the happiest and most liberally
paid of crews, and bound on a voyage that
was scarcely more than one of pleasure from
port to port.

I was as eager as any man aboard to make
an end of the voyage—to arrive, at all events,
in the South Sea, where, let the problem of
the island prove what it might, we should
have come to the end of our expectations,

and be able to see our way to the near
future, that might signify a return home for
me and Miss Temple ; and, consequently, I
never spared the barque's canvas, but, on the
contrary, would hold on every rag to the
very last, leaving the white clipper hull to
sweep through it at the pace of a comet.
The carpenter used the little ship in the same
way, and between us both, our runs in the
twenty-four hours would again and again rise
to figures that might have been deemed
almost miraculous in those days of round
bows and kettle bottoms, of apple sides, and
a beam but a third less than the length. To
be sure, when I was at sea professionally, I
was never in a position to give an order,
nor were the midshipmen, of whom I was
one, regarded as much better than inconvenient ornaments, though we were well
grounded in navigation ; yet this command
that had been forced upon me caused me no
uneasiness ; I would find myself walking the
weather side of the poop as though I had
been master of a ship for years ; I knew, or
thought I knew, exactly what to do, and the
men sprang to my orders, and the little ship
could not have been managed better had she

been handsomely officered by men grown grey in the profession, instead of commanded by a young fellow who had only passed two years at sea a long while earlier, whose chief mate was a surly and sinister old rascal, so illiterate as to be unable to read his own name when written by another, and as incapable of handling a sextant as of expressing himself in correct English.

It came into my head once that we might run short of fresh water before we should arrive at that spot on the chart where the captain's gold was supposed to be buried, and I earnestly hoped that this might happen, since a threat of thirst must infallibly drive us for help to the first port we could manage to reach. I asked the carpenter if he knew what stock of water there was aboard. He said no, but promised to find out, and later in the day came to tell me that there were so many casks, making in all so many gallons— I cannot recollect the figures. To satisfy myself, I went into the hold with him, and discovered that he was right, and then entered into a calculation, which, to my secret mortification and disappointment, expressed a sufficient quantity of water aboard to last all hands of us at a liberal supply per diem for at least six months.

Now that I had assured myself as to the posture of the crew, and was profoundly satisfied in my own mind that their consuming eagerness to arrive at the island would guarantee a uniformly proper behaviour in them, unless they addressed themselves to the rum casks, or unless I gave them cause to turn upon me, I had no misgiving in suffering Miss Temple to be seen by them. She was therefore constantly with me on deck when my lookout came round, and all the hours I could spare from sleep I dedicated to her society; so that it would be impossible to imagine any young unmarried couple passing the time in an association more intimate and incessant. At the beginning of this run to the South Pacific she showed a spirit that afterwards temporarily failed her. It was two days after I had consented to navigate the vessel that I observed a certain air of determination in her, as though she had been earnestly contemplating our situation, and had formed her resolution to encounter what might come with courage and patience. Then, after awhile, her pluck seemed to fail her again; I would find her sitting motionless in the cabin with her eyes fixed on the deck, and an expression of misery in her face, as though her heart were broken. I could not induce her to eat; though, God knows, there was little or nothing to tempt her with. She could not sleep, she told me; and the glow faded out of her deep and beautiful eyes. Pale she always was, but now her face took a character of haggardness, which her whiteness, that was a loveliness in her when in health, accentuated to a degree that was presently shocking to me. When on deck, she would take my arm and walk list-lessly, almost lifelessly, by my side, briefly replying to me in low tones, which trembled with excess of grief.

Secretly loving her as I did, though not as yet had a syllable, nay, as I believe, had a look of my passion escaped me, I began to dread the influence of her misery upon my behaviour to the men. She was a constant appeal to me, so to speak, to call the fellows aft, and tell them that the girl was pining her heart away, that she must be put ashore or conveyed aboard another ship this side Cape Horn, though it came to our backing our maintop-sail to wait for one, or that I would throw up

my command of the vessel and refuse to sail
her another mile. I say I lived in mortal
fear of my being forced into this by sentiment
and sympathy; for I was advised by every
secret instinct, by every glance I levelled at
the crew, by every look I directed at the
carpenter, that the certain issue of such a
resolution as that must involve my life!

I do not exaggerate in this; the nimble-
ness and sleekness of the crew were the
qualities of the tiger; the ferocity of the wild
beast was in them too, and for the girl's sake
I recoiled in terror from the mere fancy of
arousing their passions. How they might
serve me if I showed myself stubborn in proposals which they declined to accept, I could
not foresee; they might send me adrift in a
boat; they might more mercifully knock me
over the head in the dark, and toss what their
weapons left of me overboard. I was unalter-
ably convinced, at all events, that if I ceased
to be of use to them, then, as the possessor of
the secret of the island, I should be made
away with. But Miss Temple they would
keep with them! Of that I had no shadow of
a doubt either; and hence I say I was in
terror lest the spectacle of her misery should

impel me to some act that, even whilst it was doing, my reason would pronounce madness.

I said everything I could imagine that I thought might reassure her, and one afternoon spent two hours in earnest talk with her. I told her that her grief was influencing me, and that it might come to my not being able to control myself in my relations with the crew ; and I went on to point out what must follow if I suffered my sorrow for her to betray me into any other attitude towards the men than that I now wore. I had never been very candid in this way with her before, not choosing to excite her alarm and distress, and now I succeeded in thoroughly frightening her. It was enough that I should indicate the probability of her being left alone among the crew to fill her with horror. I need not give you the substance of my talk with her. So much remains to be told that I can only refer to it. But it achieved the end I had hoped to witness.

When next day came, I found some spirit in her voice and manner. Whilst we sat at breakfast alone, as we invariably were whether in the cuddy or on deck, she exclaimed, viewing me with an earnestness which there was

nothing in the faint smile that accompanied it
to diminish :

'I have taken your lecture to heart, Mr.
Dugdale, and I mean to reform. I have
shown myself a sad coward ; but you shall
have no further reason to complain of me for
that. I am ashamed of myself. I wonder
that I have confidence enough to look at you
when I compare my behaviour with yours.
You have thought only of me, and I have
thought only of myself ; and that is the difference between us.'

'It puts a new pulse into my heart to
hear you talk so,' said I. 'I want to conduct
you home to your mother's side out of this
wild adventure, with the same beauty and
health that you brought away from England
with you. It grieved me to the soul to see
you refusing food, to watch your face growing
hollow, to hear of your sleepless nights, and
to witness in your eyes the misery that was
consuming you. Pray keep this steadfastly
in mind—that every day shortens our run to
the South Pacific, and that every day this
horrible experience is lessened by twenty-four
hours. Whether there be gold in the island
or not, whether the island have existence or

not, the crew must still be dependent upon
me to carry them to a port, and the port that
is good for them will be good for us; for it
will be strange if from it we are unable to
proceed straight home. All along I have said
it is but a question of patience and waiting,
and God alone can tell how grateful I shall be
to you if you will enable me to play the part
that I know *must* be played if our safety is to
be worth a rushlight.'

From this time she showed herself a
thoroughly resolved woman. She ceased to
tease me with regrets, to distress me with
inquiries which I could not answer, to imply
by her silence or her sighs or looks of re-
proach that I had it in my power by some
other sort of policy than what I was pursuing,
to get her safely away out of the barque.
With this new mind in her came a subtle but
appreciable change in her manner towards
me. Heretofore her behaviour had been uniformly haunted by some small flavour more
or less defined of her treatment of me, and
indeed of all others, saving Mr. Colledge,
aboard the Indiaman. She had suggested,
though perhaps without intending it, a sort of
condescension in our quiet hours, with a deal

of haughtiness and almost contemptuous command in moments when she was wrought up
by alarm and despair. I now found a kind of
yielding in her, a compliance, a complaisance
that was almost tender, a subdued form of
expression, no matter what the mood might
be which our conversation happened to excite
in her. At times I would observe her watching me with an expression of sweetness in
her fine eyes, though these sudden discoveries
never betrayed her into the least air of confusion or embarrassment upon which I might
found a hope that I was slowly making my
way to her heart.

However, I consoled myself by thinking
that our situation hung in too black a shadow
over her mind to enable her to guess at what
might be going on in it. Besides, never a
word had I let fall that she could construe
into a revelation of my passion for her. Had
I loved her a thousandfold more than I did,
my honour must have held my emotions
dumb. It was not only that my pride determined me to keep silent until I might have
good reason to believe that my love would
not be declined by this high and mighty
young lady of the *Countess Ida*, with hidden

wonder at my impertinence in offering it; I
also was sensible that I should be acting the
meanest part in the world to let her guess my
feelings—by my language, at least; my face
I might not be always able to control—
whilst she continued in this miserable condition, utterly dependent upon me for protection, and too helpless to avow any resentment,
which she would be desperately quick to express and let me feel under other circum-
stances.

We should be entering the bitter climate
of the Horn presently, and she was without
warm apparel. Her dress, as you know, was
the light tropical costume in which she had
attired herself to visit the corvette. What
was to be done?

'You cannot face the weather of the Horn
in that garb,' said I on one occasion, lightly
glancing at her dress, to which her noble and
faultless figure communicated a grace that
the wear and tear and soiling of the many
days she had worn it could not rob it of.
'Needs must, you know, when Old Nick
drives. There is but one expedient; I hope
you will not make a grimace at it.'

'Tell it to me?'

'There is a good, warm, long pilot coat in my cabin. I will borrow needles and thread, and you must go to work to make it fit you.'

She laughed with a slight blush. 'I fear I shall not be able to manage it.'

'Try. If you fail, fifty to one but that there is some man forward who will contrive it for you. Most sailors can sew and cut out after a fashion. But I would rather you should try your hand at it alone. If I employ a fellow forward he will have to come aft and measure you, and so on ; all of which I don't want.'

'Nor I,' she cried eagerly. 'I will try the coat on now, Mr. Dugdale. I daresay I shall be able to fashion it into some sort of jacket,' she added with another laugh that trembled with a sigh.

I procured the coat, and helped her to put it on. It had been built for an overcoat, and designed to wrap up more than the narrow shoulders for which it had been fashioned, and it buttoned easily over the girl's swelling figure.

'Come, we shan't want a tailor after all,'

said I, backing a step to admire her in this
new, queer apparel.

'It will keep me warm,' said she, turning
about to take a view of herself.

'And now,' said I, 'for a hat. That
elegant straw of yours will not do for Cape
Horn.

I overhauled the captain's wardrobe, and
unearthed three hats of different kinds—one
of them a wideawake; another, a cap of some
kind of skin, very good to keep a night-watch
in in dirty weather; and the third, an old-
fashioned tarpaulin glazed hat—the sire of
the sou'-wester of our own times, though, to
be sure, sou'-wester caps, as they were called,
were in use at the beginning of the century.
This example of head-gear I returned to the
locker in which I had found it, but the other
two Miss Temple thought she could make
serviceable. She tried them on, stealing
glances almost coquettish at me as she peered
at herself in the looking-glass which I brought
from her cabin.

There had been a time when nothing, I
am persuaded, could have induced her to
touch those hats. She would have shrunk
from them with the aversion and disgust she

had exhibited at Captain Braine's suggestions about the furnishing of her cabin in the steerage. Assuredly, old ocean was working a mighty change in her character. Life real, stern, uncompromising, was busy with her ; and just as Byron says of his shipwrecked people, that the mothers of them would not have known their own sons, so was I assured of my shipmate Louise that if it pleased God we should escape from the perils of this adventure, she would emerge a changed woman in every characteristic that had been displeasing in her before.

CHAPTER XXXVI

I CONVERSE WITH WETHERLY

Not to dwell too long on a detail of insigni-
ficance, it will suffice to say that by dint of
rummaging the wardrobes of Captain Braine
and Mr. Chicken I obtained several useful
articles, and Miss Temple went to work to
convert them into wearing-apparel for herself,
with the help of a pair of scissors which I
borrowed from the carpenter, and needles and
thread procured from amongst the men by
Wetherly. The occupation was useful to
her in other ways; it killed the tedious, the
insufferably tedious time, and it gave her
something to think of, and even something to
look forward to, so blank had been the hours.

I remember coming out of my cabin after
a spell of sleep to take sights shortly before
noon, and finding her seated at the table with
some flannel or fine blanket stuff before her,
at which she was stitching—ripped up and

violated vestments of either Braine or Chicken, but brand-new, or she would scarcely have meddled with them. She received me with a smile and a few words, and then went on sewing with an air as of gratification in her that I should have found her at work.

I halted, and stood looking on, feigning to watch her busy fingers, whilst in reality I gazed at her face with a lover's delight. It was hard to believe that what was passing was something more than a dream, astonishingly vivid and logical. Again and again, when in the company of this girl, a sense of the unreality of our association had possessed me to such a degree at times that had the feeling continued, I might honestly have feared for my head. But never before this moment had that sense been so strong upon me. I forgot her beauty in my wonder. It was sheer bewilderment to recall her as she was on board the Indiaman; her haughtiness, her disdain, her contemptuous insensibility to all presences save that of my Lord Sandown's son, the cold glance of scornful surprise that would instantly cause me to avert mine—to recall this and how much more? and behold her now pensively bending her lovely head

and face of high-bred charms over that sordid
need of rough sailor's clothes, occasionally
stealing a peep at me of mingled sweetness
and a sort of wistful amusement, as though
she grieved while she smiled at the necessity
that had brought her to such a pass. Yet
there was no repining; if she sighed, it was
under her breath; forced as her light air of
cheerfulness might be, it proved a growing
resolution of spirit, a development of heroic
forces, latent in her till recently.

Secretly, however, I was worried by keen
anxiety. What was to be the issue of this
voyage? I merely feigned a manner of confidence when talking with her about the result
of this amazing ramble, as I chose to figure
it. In reality, I could not think of the time
when we should have arrived upon the spot
where the dead captain had declared his
island to be without dread. Suppose there
were no island! What next step would the
men take? The disappointment that must
follow their long dream of gold might determine them upon plundering the barque—put
them upon some wild scheme of converting
her and her cargo into money. Or suppose
—though I never seriously considered the

matter thus—suppose, I would ask myself,
that the island proved real, that the treasure
proved real, that the men should dig and
actually find the gold! What then? Was
I to conceive that a body of ignorant, reck-
less, lawless sailors, led by a man who was at
heart the completest imaginable copy of a
sea-villain, would peaceably divide the treasure
amongst them, pay me over my share—which,
God knows, I should have been willing to
attach to Mr. Lush's feet on condition of the
others throwing him overboard—and suffer
me to quietly navigate the barque to an adjacent port, conscious that I owed them a bitter
grudge for the outrage they had committed
in forcing me and the lady to accompany
them?

At long intervals I would exchange a few
sentences with Joe Wetherly. Unfortunately,
he was in the carpenter's watch, and my
opportunities, therefore, for speaking with
him were few. It was only now and again,
when he was required to keep a lookout for
Lush or myself, that I contrived to gather
what was going forward amongst the men by
engaging him in a brief chat before he quitted
the poop. I was so sensible of being keenly

observed by all hands, that I was obliged to
exercise the utmost caution in speaking to
this man. On the poop there was always the
fellow at the helm to observe me; and the
quarter-deck was within the easy reach of men
stirring about the galley, or leaving or
entering the forecastle.

However, it happened one dog-watch that
Wetherly came aft instead of the carpenter
to relieve me. Mr. Lush, he told me, felt
unwell, and had asked him to stand his watch
from eight to twelve. It was a clear night,
but dark, the south-east trade-wind strong off
the port beam, and the weather dry and cold,
with a frosty glitter in the trembling of the
stars which enriched the heavens with such a
multitude of white and green lights that the
firmament seemed to hover over our mastheads like some vast sheet of black velvet
gloriously spangled with brilliants and
emeralds and dust of diamonds and tender
miracles of delicate prisms.

Miss Temple had left me some twenty
minutes or so, and was now in the cabin,
seated at the table under the lamp, with a
pencil in her hand, with which she drew outlines upon a sheet of paper with an air of

profound absent-mindedness. She wore over her dress a knitted waistcoat that had belonged to the captain ; it stretched to her figure, and it was already a need even in the day-time with the sun shining brightly, for we were penetrating well to the southwards, and every score of miles which the nimble keel of the barque could measure made a sensible difference in the temperature of even the shelter in the cabin. It was too dark to distinguish Wetherly until he was close. On hearing that he was to keep the deck until twelve, I determined to have a long chat with him, to get with some thoroughness at his views, which, to a certain extent, I had found a bit puzzling, and to gather what information I could from him touching the behaviour I might expect in the crew if there should be no gold, or, which was the same, no island.

The fellow who had come to the wheel at eight bells was Forrest, the supple, piratic-looking young sailor, whose walk, as he rolled along the lee-deck, his figure swinging against the stars over the rail, had told me who he was without need of my going to the binnacle to make sure. Whilst Wetherly talked about the carpenter feeling unwell, I drew him aft,

that we might be within earshot of Forrest,
and said, as I turned to the companion hatch:
'I'll bring my pipe on deck, Wetherly, for a
smoke after I've had a bite below. I wish to
keep an eye upon the weather till two bells.
Those green stars to wind'ard may signify
more than a mere atmospheric effect.'

'Ay, ay, sir,' he answered in a voice that
made me see that he took my words in their
most literal meaning.

I remained below until half-past eight,
talking with Miss Temple, eating a little
supper, and so on. I then fetched my pipe,
and told her that I should be down again at
nine, and that I did not ask her to accompany
me, as I wished to have a talk with Wetherly.
She fixed her dark eyes upon me with an
expression of inquiry, but asked no questions.
There had been a time when she would have
opened the full battery of her alarm and
anxiety upon me, but silence was now become
a habit with her. It was her confession of
faith in my judgment, an admission that she
expected no other information than such as I
chose to give her. I cannot express how this
new behaviour was emphasised by the eloquence of her beauty, in which I could witness

the curiosity and the apprehension which she had disciplined her tongue to suppress.

I left her, and went on deck. I first walked to the binnacle, into which I peered, and then in the sheen of it gazed very earnestly to windward and around, as though I was a little uneasy. The floating figure of Forrest swayed at the wheel, and I observed that he cast several glances to windward also. Muttering to myself, as though thinking aloud, 'Those green stars show uncommonly bright!' I went abruptly to the break of the poop, where the dark form of Wetherly was pacing, as though my mind were full of the weather.

'What's wrong with them stars, sir, d'ye think?' said he.

'Oh, nothing in the world,' I answered. 'They are very honest trade-wind stars. I wanted an excuse for a chat, Wetherly. Forrest has the ears of a prairie hunter. I'm not here to talk to you about the weather. You are the only man on board in whom I can confide. As we approach the Horn, my anxieties gain upon me. How is this voyage to end? By this time you pretty well understand the disposition of the crew. If there should be no island, what then, Wetherly?'

I noticed a cautious pause in him.

'Mr. Dugdale,' he answered, 'I'm heartily consarned for you, and for the lady too, and I may say particularly for the lady, who seems to me to be a born princess, a sight too good for such quarters as them'—he pointed to the skylight with a shadowy hand—'with naught but a dead man's clothes to keep her warm. If I could be of sarvice to ye, I would; but I've got to be as careful as you. Mr. Lush has such a hold upon the minds of the crew that there's nothen he couldn't get 'em to do, I believe; and if he should come to suspect that there's anything 'twixt you and me, any sort of confidence that aint direct in the interests of the fo'c'sle, it 'ud go as hard with me as I may tell 'ee it certainly would with *you* if you was to play 'em false.'

This speech he delivered in a low key, with frequent glances aft and at the quarter-deck below. I listened with patience, though he told me nothing that I was not fully aware of.

'But what course, Wetherly, do you think these men will adopt if on our arrival at the latitude and longitude named by that unhappy madman as the spot where his treasure lies, there should be no island?'

'Well, sir,' he responded, preserving his cautious tone, 'I can answer that question, for it's formed a part of the consultations the crew is agin and agin a-holding. They'll think ye've dished 'em, and that o' purpose you han't steered a true course.'

'Ha!' I exclaimed; 'and what then?'

'You'll have to find the island, sir.'

'But, my God, Wetherly, if it be not there! There is no rock marked on the chart in the place that was named by Captain Braine.'

'They'll keep ye a-hunting for it,' said he grimly.

'And if we don't find it?'

'Well, I can't tell 'ee *what* they'll do. All they've said is, "If it ain't there, it'll be because he don't mean it shall be." But I've heard no threats—no talk of what 'ud follow.'

'If there should be no gold, no island,' said I, 'my opinion is that they will seize upon the ship and cargo, and compel me to navigate her to some port where they will find a market for their plunder.'

'And where will that be?' he asked.

'Impossible to say. Lush will probably know. He has the airs and appearance of a man to whom a performance of the kind I suggest would be no novelty. I may tell you now, Wetherly, and, indeed, I might have done so long ago, that it was the carpenter whom Captain Braine charged with murder.'

'Well, sir, you'll excuse me. I'm not for believing that, Mr. Dugdale. That Lush has been a rare old sinner, ye need only watch him by daylight and hear him talk in his sleep at night, to know ; but, as I said afore, when ye mentioned it—murder '—I saw him wag his head by the starlight—' I'd choose to make sure afore believing it on the evidence of a madman.'

'But don't you think the carpenter and, let me add, most of the crew equal to the commission of any crime ? '

'Well, I won't say no to that now with this here glittering temptation of money getting into their souls, to work everything that may be evil in 'em out through their skins. I wouldn't trust 'em, and so I tell 'ee, Mr. Dugdale ; and if this here barque was any other ship than the *Lady Blanche*, and my mates any other men but what they are, I'd be content to pawn for sixpence all that I've got in my chest.'

I came to a stand with him for a while at the weather rail in feigned contemplation of the weather.

' Wetherly,' said I quietly, as we resumed our crosswise walk, ' my position is a frightful one. Were it not for the cursed lunatic fancy that that shambling villain Wilkins overheard —the completest lie that ever took shape in a madman's brain—I might hope to be able to tempt the crew with a handsome reward to allow me to sail this ship to a port whence the lady and I could get home. But what could I offer, with honest intention to pay, that should approach the thousands which those fools yonder dream about day and night?'

He made no answer.

' Supposing, Wetherly,' I continued, ' I should determine, in a mood of desperation, to drop my command here, and refuse to navigate the vessel another league unless Miss Temple and I are put ashore?'

' You know what 'ud happen,' he cried; ' ye've said it o'er and o'er agin, hitting upon what's most likely. For God's sake, sir, clear your mind o' that scheme, if it's only for the lady's sake ! '

'But what's to follow upon our arrival in the Pacific ? ' I exclaimed with an emotion of despair.

' There's nothen to be done but to wait,' he answered gloomily.

' Do you believe that every mother's son forward believes in the existence of the treasure ? '

' Every mother's son of 'em, sir. The belief mightn't have been so general, I daresay, if it hadn't been for them documents you signed. Ignorant as the men are, they know how to git four out of two and two. First, there's the drawing on that there bit of parchment ; then there was the capt'n's yarn of how he come by the gold, as ship-shape to the minds of the men as if they'd seen him fetch it out of the Bank of England ; then comes the plot of getting rid of 'em at Rio, with a crew of Kanakas to follow ; and then a company of beachcombers atop of them, to carry the barque on. Here alone's a thought-out scheme proper to convince an atheist. But then follows them documents o' yourn to prove that you, a born gent of eddication and first-class intelligence, don't doubt the truth o' what ye hear, and, to make sure, provide for your share when the gold's come at and for your security, if so be as the law should lay hold on the capt'n for a-deviating.'

'It's all very true,' I exclaimed, staggered myself by the consistency of the wretched business, and forced to mentally admit the reasonableness of the illiterate creatures in the forecastle accepting it all as indisputable. 'But you know my motive in acting as I did?'

'Well, I *do*, sir. As I told ye, I was a bit nonplushed at first; but it's a madman's yarn—ne'er a doubt of it. And I'm as wishful, Mr. Dugdale, as ever ye can be to be quit of the whole blooming job.'

Again I came to a pause at the weather rail, as though I lingered on deck only to observe the weather.

'Now, Wetherly, listen to me,' said I. 'You know you are the only man in the ship that I would dream of opening my lips to. You have my full confidence; I believe you to be sound to the core. If you will give me your word I shall be perfectly satisfied that you will not betray me.'

'Whatever ye may tell me, Mr. Dugdale,' he responded in a voice slightly agitated, 'I swear to keep locked up in my bosom; but afore I can give ye my word, I must know what I've got to take my oath on.'

'You misunderstand me,' I exclaimed; 'I desire no oath. Simply assure me that should a time ever come when I may see my way to escape, you will stand my friend; you will actively assist me if you can—you will not be neutral; I mean, merely my well-wisher; simply tell me this, and I shall know that when an opportunity arises, I will have you to count upon.'

'Have you a scheme, first of all, Mr. Dugdale?' he inquired. 'There's no good in my consenting to anything that's agoing to end in getting our throats cut.'

'No; I have no scheme. What plan could I form? I must grasp the first, the best chance that offers, and then it may be that I will want you. There are others besides myself whom you would find grateful. Miss Temple's mother is a lady of title, and a rich woman '——

'Excuse me, Mr. Dugdale,' he interrupted; 'I don't want no bribe to bring me into a proper way of acting, if so be as that proper

way ain't a-going to cost too much. I'll say
downright, now, that if I can help you and the
lady to get out of this job and put ye both in
the road of getting home, ye may depend upon
my doing my best. More'n that there'd be
no use in saying, seeing that it ain't possible
to consart a scheme, and that we must wait
until something tarns up. If there be an island,
and we bring up off it, the sort of opportunity
you want may come, and you'll find all of me
there. If the island be a delusion, then something else 'll have to be waited for. But I tell
you as man to man that I'm with you and
the lady, that I don't like Mr. Lush nor the
business he's brought the vessel's crew into
but that I've got to be as cautious as you;
which now means, sir—and I beg that you'll
onderstand me as speaking respectfully—that
that there Forrest has seen us together long
enough.'

'Right,' I exclaimed, grasping his hand;
'I thank you from my heart for your assurance; and Miss Temple shall thank you
herself.'

With which I went aft, gazing steadfastly
to windward as I walked, and after a final

peep into the binnacle and a slow look round,
I stepped below.

There was little to comfort me in this chat
with Wetherly; it was worth knowing, however, that he regarded the captain's yarn as a
mere emission of craziness; for heretofore, in
the few conversations I had had with him, his
hesitation, his cautious inquiries, his manner,
that in a superior person would to a certain
extent have suggested irony, had caused me
to see that his mind was by no means made
up on the subject. This, then, was to the
good, and it was satisfactory to be informed
by him that he would befriend us if an opportunity occurred, providing his assistance should
not jeopardise his life. I was grateful for this
promise, but scarcely comforted by it. I
carried a clouded face into the cabin; Miss
Temple, who awaited my return to the cabin,
fixed an anxious gaze upon me, but asked no
questions.

'How good you are to suppress your
curiosity!' I exclaimed, standing by her side,
and looking into her upturned face; 'you
incalculably lighten my burthen by your for-
bearance.'

'You have taught me my lesson,' she

answered quietly ; ' and as a pupil I should be proud of the commendations of my master.' She pronounced the word ' master ' with a glance of her proud eyes through the droop of the lashes, and a smile at once sweet and haughty played upon her lips.

'It will comfort you to know that Wetherly is our friend,' said I.

'I have always regarded him as so,' she responded.

'Yes; but he has now consented to aid me in any effort I may by-and-by make to escape with you from this barque.'

She was silent, but her face was eloquent with nervous eager questioning.

'Moreover,' I proceeded, 'Wetherly is now convinced that Captain Braine's gold was a dream of that man's madness. A dream of course it is. But do you know I am extremely anxious that we should find an island in that latitude and longitude of waters to which I shall be presently heading this ship.'

'May I ask why?'

'Because I think—mind, I do but think— that I may see a way to escape with you and Wetherly alone in this barque.' She breathed quickly, and watched me with impassioned attention. 'In fact,' I continued, 'even as I stand here, looking at you, Miss Temple, a resolution grows in me to create an island for Captain Braine's gold, should the bearings he gave me prove barren of land.'

'Create?' she exclaimed musingly.

'Yes. The South Sea is full of rocks. I'll find the men a reef, and that reef must provide me with my chance. But,' I exclaimed, breaking off and looking at my watch, 'it is time for me to seek some rest. I shall have to be on deck again at twelve.'

'I shall go to bed also,' she exclaimed; 'it is dull—and there are many weeks before us yet.' She smiled with a quivering lip, as though she would have me know that she rebuked herself for complaining. 'I believe you would tell me more if you had the least faith in my judgment.'

'At present, I have nothing to tell; but an hour may come when I shall have to depend very largely upon your judgment and your spirit also.'

She met my eyes with a firm, full, glowing gaze. 'No matter what task you assign to me,' she cried with vehemence, 'you will find me equal to it. This life is insupportable; and

I would choose at this instant the chance of death side by side with the chance of escape, sooner than continue as I am in this horrible condition of uncertainty, banishment, and misery.'

'That may be the spirit I shall want to evoke,' I said, smiling, whilst I held open her cabin door. 'Good-night, Miss Temple.'

She held my hand a moment or two before relinquishing it. 'I hope I have said nothing to vex you, Mr. Dugdale?' she exclaimed, slightly inclining her fine head into a posture that might make one think of a princess expressing an apology.

'What have *I* said that you should think so?' I answered.

'Your manner is a little hard,' she exclaimed in a low voice.

'God forgive me if it be so,' said I. 'Not to you, Miss Temple, would I be hard.'

My voice trembled as I pronounced these words, and abruptly I caught up her hand and pressed her fingers to my lips, and bowing, closed the door upon her and entered my own berth.

CHAPTER XXXVII

CAPE HORN

It was on one of the closing days of the month of December that my longitude being then some three leagues east of the easternmost of the Falkland Islands, and my latitude some fifty-five degrees south, that I brought the barque's head to a west-south-west course for the rounding of Cape Horn. It was happily the summer season in those parts—their midsummer, indeed—and I was glad to believe that the horrors of this passage would be mitigated by a sun that in the month of June shines for scarcely six hours in the day over the ice-laden surge of this, the most inhospitable, the most bitterly dreary tract of waters upon the face of the world.

Down to the latitude of the Falkland Islands we had sighted, from the hour of my taking command of the barque, but four sail, so vast is the ocean, and so minute a speck

does a ship make upon it. But whilst the
loom of the land about Berkeley Sound was
hanging in a blue and windy shadow, with a
gleam as of snow upon it away out upon our
starboard beam, we fell in with a whaler, a
vessel rigged as ours was; a round-bowed,
motherly old craft, jogging along under a
load of boats suspended over her sides from
the extremities of thick wooden davits. There
was a long Atlantic swell running, and as she
rose and rolled to it, she showed a line of
green sheathing dark with moss and barnacles
and lines of trailing weeds.

She had been visible at daybreak right
ahead, and she was clear upon the sea over
our bow, when I came on deck shortly after
eight bells to relieve Lush, who had had the
watch since four o'clock.

'What have we there?' said I, bringing
Braine's old leather telescope out of the companion and putting my eye to it. 'A squab
old whaler, as I may suppose by her boats;
Cape Horn topgallant-masts; a sawed-off
square sea-wagon after the true Nantucket
pattern.'

'I've been a-waiting for you to come on
deck,' said the carpenter. 'We don't want

to run her down. We've got nothen to say
to her, and so 'ud better keep out of hail.
Shift the course, will you, sir?'

There was nothing in the *sir* to qualify the
offensive tone of ·command with which he
addressed me. I looked at him fixedly, taking
care, however, to keep a good grip on my
temper.

'What are you afraid of?' I asked. 'Are
any of the crew likely to hail her if we pass
within speaking distance?'

'I'd like to know what man there is
amongst us as 'ud have the courage to do it,'
he exclaimed, his face darkening to the
thought, and his eyes travelling up and down
my body, as though in search of some part on
which to settle.

'Why do you wait for me to shift the
helm, man?' said I.

'The navigation's in your hands,' he
answered sullenly; 'if your calculations don't
turn out correct, it musn't be because of any
man a-meddling with the course whilst you
was below.'

Miss Temple at this moment arrived on
deck and joined me.

'A pity to run away,' said I; 'we're sail-

ing three feet to that chap's one, and will be
passing him like smoke. There's been nothing
to look at for a long time. It'll be a treat to
our shore-going eyes to see a strange face,
though we catch but a glimpse. You don't
think *I'll* hail her, I hope?'

'*I* hope!' he responded with a coarse
ironical sneer and a rude stare of suspicion.

'By God, then!' said I, with an effusion of
temper I instantly regretted, ' since you have
forced this command upon me, I'll take what
privileges it confers, and be hanged to it!
My orders are to keep the ship as she goes.
If you disobey me, I'll call the crew aft, and
charge them to observe that any miscalcula-
tions in my navigation will be owing to your
interference.'

The fellow scowled, and looked ahead at the
vessel, and then at a knot of sailors who were
standing at the galley, and I could see that
he was at a loss ; in fact, a minute after, never
having spoken a word, during which time he
frequently sent his gaze at the craft over the
bow, he abruptly crossed to the lee side of
the deck and fell to patrolling, coming now
and again to a stand to leeward of the sailor
at the helm, with whom he would exchange

a few words, whilst he swayed on his rounded
shanks, with his arms folded upon his breast,
occasionally stooping to obtain a view of the
whaler under the curve of the fore-course.

It was his watch below, and at another
time he would have promptly gone forward.
His remaining on deck signified an insulting
menace, an impudent threat to watch me,
and to guard his own and the crew's interests
against me. But I was resolved not to seem
to notice his behaviour, nor even to appear
conscious of his presence. We were carrying
a grand sailing wind out of the south, and
under a main top-gallant sail and a boarded
main tack, the barque was sweeping nobly
over the powerful heave of the long Pacific
swell, and through the tall surges which were
breaking in foam far as the eye could reach,
with deep blue lines between. At intervals,
some great hill of waters sparkling to the
flying sunshine would flash into foam to the
buoyant rise of the glittering metalled fore-
foot of the speeding, milk-white fabric, and
cloud her forecastle in a storm of snow. The
wind sang in the rigging with a frosty note,
but the shrewd air was dry, without any
sting of ice, though there was no warmth

whatever in the white splendour of the leaping sun.

The men observing that Lush kept the deck, came out of the galley and forecastle, and with abrupt shifting motions gradually drew aft to the line of the quarter-deck rail, which they overhung, feigning to watch the ship we were overtaking, though nothing could be more obvious than their real motive in drawing aft in this fashion. Wetherly alone kept forward. He stood leaning in the galley door, smoking a short pipe in as careless and unconcerned a posture as you would look to see in a lounging fellow sailing up the river Thames.

'The brutes are terribly in earnest,' said I to Miss Temple, as we stood together under the lee of the weather quarter-boat for the shelter of it. 'If ever I had had a doubt of the wisdom of my conduct in this business, the presence of that group yonder would extinguish it for good and all.'

'Forgive me,' she exclaimed; 'but were you well advised in not altering the course of this vessel?'

'The fellows must not know that I am

afraid of them, or believe me to be without some resolution of character.'

'What would happen were you to attempt to hail that ship there?' she asked, with her eyes enlarging to the fear that accompanied the question, and her lips quivering as they closed to a blast of wind sweeping in a long howl betwixt the rail and the keel of the boat.

'I do not intend to hail her,' I replied; 'and we will not, therefore, distract our minds with conjectures. Let us rather wonder,' I went on, forcing a light air of cheerfulness upon me, 'what those whalemen will think of you when they catch a sight of your figure? Will they take you to be captain or chief mate?'

She smiled, and slightly coloured. Indeed, at a little distance, with the rail to hide her dress, she would very well have passed for a young man, habited as she was in Captain Braine's long pilot coat and his wide-awake, which entirely hid her hair to the level of her ears, and which she kept seated on her head by means of a piece of black tape passed under her chin. But shall I tell you that her beauty borrowed a new and fascinating freshness of grace from the very oddity of her attire? For my part, I found her more admirable in the perfections of her face and form, grotesquely clothed as she was, than had she come to my side but now from the hands of the most fashionable dressmaker and the most modish of hairdressers and milliners.

The name of the old whaler lifted clear in long white letters to the heave of her square stern off the spread of froth that raced from under her counter: *Maria Jane Taylor* was her title, and I remember it now as I can remember very much smaller matters which entered into that abominable time. The green and weedy and rust-stained fabric, heeling to the pressure of the wind, and making prodigious weather of the Pacific surge as she crushed into the violet hollow with a commotion of foam such as no whale which ever her boats had made fast to could have raised in its death-agony, swarmed and staggered along with frequent wild slantings of her spars, upon which her ill-patched sails pulled in disorderly spaces. A whole mob of people, black, orange-coloured, and white, stared at us from under all kinds of singular headgear over her weather rail, and a man

swinging off in the mizzen shrouds, apparently
waited for us to come abreast to hail us. As
our clipper keel swept in thunder to her
quarter, scarcely more water than a pistol-
shot could measure dividing us, Lush came
up from to leeward and stood beside me, but
without speaking, simply holding himself in
readiness—as I might witness in the sulky
determined expression in the villain's face—
to silence me if I should attempt to hail. I
glanced at him askant, running my eye down
his round-backed muscular figure, and then
put on a behaviour of perfect insensibility to
his presence.

'How touching is the sight of a strange
face,' said I to Miss Temple, ' encountered in
the heart of such a waste as this! Rough as
those fellows are, how could one take them
by the hand! with what pleasure could one
listen to their voices! Would to God we
were aboard of her!' And I brought my
foot with a stamp of momentary poignant
impatience to the deck.

Our own crew staring at the whaler over
the quarter-deck bulwarks were incessantly
bringing their eyes away from her to fix them
upon me with a manner of angry suspicion

that it was impossible to mistake. The noise of the roaring of the wind in her canvas was loud in the pouring air; the blue waters foamed viciously to her tall catheads, and her green and rusty bends showed raggedly amid the frothing, foaming, and seething curves of the boiling smother rushing past her; here and there aft was the muddy glint of a disc of begrimed window amid the line of her seams, out of which all the caulking appeared to have dropped. We were passing her as a roll of smoke might.

'Barque ahoy!' bawled the long slab-sided man in the mizzen rigging in the nasal accents of the 'longshore Yankee.

Lush at my side stood grimly staring. Several of the crew on the quarter-deck were now watching me continuously.

'What barque air you?' came in a hurricane note out of the whaler's mizzen shrouds.

There was no reply from us.

'Barque ahoy, I say!' yelled the man with a frantic gesture of astonishment; 'where air you bound, and what ship might you be?'

The *Lady Blanche* rushed on; nevertheless, we were yet so close to the whaler even

when we had her on our quarter that I could
easily distinguish the features of the man who
had hailed us as he hung motionless, as though
withered by some blast from the skies, in the
mizzen rigging, with his mouth wide open,
whilst an expression of inimitable amazement
was visible in the rows of faces along the
bulwark rail, white and coloured alternately,
like the keys of a pianoforte.

On a sudden the man sprang out of the
mizzen shrouds on to the deck; his legs were
immensely long, and he was habited in a short
monkey jacket. He started to run for the
forecastle, and his prodigious strides made
one think of a pair of tongs put into motion
by some electrical power. He gained the
forecastle head, where for one moment he
stood surveying us, then bringing his hands
to his face, he made what is known to school-
boys as a 'long-nose' at us, turning a little
sideways, that we might clearly observe the
humiliating derisiveness of his posture. In
this attitude he remained whilst a man might
have counted twenty, then turning his back
upon us, he smote himself with a gesture of
utmost scorn upon a part of his body which
the short skirts of his monkey jacket left par-

tially exposed; after which, with the air of a
person whose mind has been relieved, he
leisurely made his way aft, thrice, as he
walked, turning his profile, that we might
observe him lift his thumb and fingers again
to his nose. A little while later the old
whaler was plunging amid the white throb-
bings of her own churning a long mile astern;
and in half an hour she looked to be scarcely
more than a gleam out in the cold blue air,
where there seemed a dimness in the atmosphere as of the blowing of crystals off the
melting heads of the high seas.

It was not till then that Lush left the
deck.

This little incident was as stern a warrant
of the disposition of the crew as they could
have desired to make me understand. It
proved their possession of a quality of suspicion, of a character so ungovernably insolent
and daring, that I might well believe, were it
transformed into passion by disappointment
or insincerity on my part, there was no infamy
it would not render them equal to. I often
wonder in recalling this time that I should
have found strength to bear up under my
anxieties. The future lay absolutely in black-

ness. I had some hope, some vague fancy, rather, let me call it, of lighting upon an island, should Braine's prove the chimera I feared it was, that might enable me to contrive a stratagem to effect our deliverance from this unspeakable situation. But there was nothing in such an imagination as this to cast the faintest light upon the gloom ahead. I would cudgel my brains in my lonely watches at night with vehement struggles in search of any idea that might be shaped into a method of escape. At intervals I would secretly and warily converse with Wetherly; but he had no other proposals to make than the soul-depressing one of patience, with regular assurances, indeed, that he would stand by me if his help could be safely ventured.

In these despairful considerations I even went to the length of fixing my thoughts upon the boats. When we should have rounded the Horn and entered the mild parallels of the Pacific, sparkling nights of tranquillity were sure to descend upon us, and furnish me with an opportunity of leaving the barque with Miss Temple; an opportunity, I say, so far as the weather and the peace of the sea might be concerned; but how with my single pair of hands was I to lower a boat, provide that Miss Temple should be in her, provide also that the little fabric should be stored with food and water, then unhook her, and slide away into the gloom, all so privily, all so noiselessly as to elude the vigilance of the man at the helm and of the seamen in my own watch sprawling about the decks forward?

It was not to be done. I did not even suggest this method of deliverance to Wetherly, feeling perfectly convinced that he would not entertain it. And suppose I should be able to successfully get away with the girl in this manner, how dreadful would be our outlook! with oars, indeed, but without masts or sails, lying exposed for God alone could tell how long a time in the heart of one of old ocean's mightiest deserts, not traversed then, as in these days; scarcely penetrated, indeed, save at long times between, by such a whaler as we had passed, or by some vessel trading to the Polynesian groups from the western South American seaboard.

I do not know that I considered myself very fortunate because of the fine weather which attended the barque in her passage of the Horn. Far better, I sometimes thought, than the strong southerly breeze, the flying skies of dark winter blue, the brilliant rolling and foaming of long arrays of billows brimming in cream to the ivory white sides of the little ship, and aiding her headlong flight with floating buoyant liftings and fallings that timed the measures of her nimble sea-dance with her waving mastheads as the batôn of a band conductor keeps the elbows of his fiddlers quivering in unison—far better might it have been for us, I would often think, had the month been the mid-winter of the Horn, with heavy westerly gales to oppose our entrance into the Pacific Ocean, and fields of ice to hinder us yet, with some disaster on top to force us to bear away as the wind might permit for the nearest port.

The rounding of this iron headland was absolutely uneventful ; the wind blew almost continuously from the southward, and throughout was a strong and steady breeze, that enabled me to show whole topsails and a maintopgallant-sail to it. Once only did we sight ice, a distant spot of a luminous crystalline whiteness upon the throbbing limits of the sea. Day and night the water in white

clouds poured in thunder from either bow of
the rushing barque ; the clouds soaring from
out the Antarctic solitudes down behind the
ocean line, swept in smoke athwart our
trucks ; by day the small white sun danced
amongst these fleeting shadows in the north,
and flashed up the sea into a very dazzle at
each blinding launch of his beams, so multi-
tudinous were the peaks of froth which
glanced back the sparkling emissions of the
luminary ; by night the dark skies were filled
with stars of a frosty brilliance, amid which
burned the jewels of the Southern Cross with
the Magellanic clouds beyond dim as curls of
vapour. A fire was lighted in the little stove
in the cabin, and by it, during my watch
below, Miss Temple and I would sit exchang-
ing our hopes and fears, speculating upon the
future, endeavouring to animate each other
with representations of our feelings when we
should have arrived home, and amid safety
and comfort look back upon the unutterable
experiences into which we had been plunged
by so trifling a circumstance as a visit to a
wreck.

Thus passed the time. Every day I obtained a clear sight of the sun, and then

striking the meridian of 76° West, I headed the barque on a north-north-west course for Captain Braine's island, the declared situation of which I calculated would occupy us about three weeks to reach.

It was on the afternoon of the day on which I had shifted the barque's helm, that Wilkins came to me as I sat at dinner with Miss Temple with a message from the carpenter to the effect that he would be glad of a word with me. I answered that I was at Mr. Lush's disposal when I had dined, but not before. This did not occupy another ten minutes in accomplishing ; my companion then withdrew to her cabin, having with much eagerness expressed a number of conjectures as to the carpenter's motive in soliciting an interview.

The man came off the poop by way of the quarter-deck and entered the cabin with his skin cap in hand.

' I observe,' said he, ' that you've altered the vessel's course.'

'That is so,' I rejoined. ' Wetherly was on deck when I left my cabin after working out my sights, and I believed he would have reported the change of course to you.'

'No; it was Woodward [one of the sailors] that was at the hellum. He calls me over and points into the binnacle and says: "Ye see what's happened?" The men 'ud be glad to know if it's all right?'

'If what is all right?'

'Why, if this here course is true for the island? They'll feel obliged if ye'll let 'em in here and show 'em the chart and 'splain the distance and the course and the likes of that to 'em yourself.'

I hardly required him to inform me of their wishes, for I had but to direct my glance at the cabin door to observe them assembled on the quarter-deck awaiting the invitation the carpenter had come to demand; all hands of them, saving Wetherly and the fellow that was steering, called Woodward by Lush.'

'Certainly: let them enter,' said I; and at once fetched my chart, which I placed upon the table, and went to the other side, ruler in hand, ready to point and to explain.

The body of rough men, a few of them with their mahogany lineaments scarcely visible amidst the whiskers, eyebrows, and falls of front hair which obscured their countenances, stood looking upon the chart with Lush in the thick of them, and Forrest's mutinous, dare-devil, rolling face conspicuous over the carpenter's shoulder.

' Now, men, what is it you want to know? ' said I.

' We're a steering by the compass up above nor'-nor'-west,' answered Lush ; ' will ye be pleased to tell us how ye make that right ? '

I had to fetch a pair of parallel rulers to render my answer intelligible to the illiterate creatures who stood gaping at me with an expression of dull struggling perception that would come and go in a manner that must have moved me to laughter at another time.

' What part of this here paper is the island wrote down upon? ' demanded Forrest.

I pointed with my ruler, and the whole knot of faces came together as they stooped with a sound as of a general snore arising from their vigorous breathing.

' How far is it off from where we are? ' inquired one of the men. I told him. Several questions of a like kind were put to me ; a growling ran amongst them as they hummed their comments into one another's ears. Meanwhile, I stood inspecting them with mingled inquisitiveness and disgust. What a miserable pass had the wretches brought the girl and me to! What bitter anxieties had they overwhelmed us with! What was to be our future so far as they should have a share in the creation of it? I sought in vain amidst their various countenances, composed of hair and warts and beards, of leathery skins, of moist eyes dim with weather, of the smooth cheeks of two or three of the younger fellows— I sought in vain, I say, for a single expression to assure me of the existence of qualities upon whose generous response I might depend, should it ever come to my having to entreat them. Yet they presented, as I long ago said, just such exteriors as you would expect to meet with in the sailors of a humble trader like the *Lady Blanche*.

'Well, men,' exclaimed the carpenter, 'there ain't no doubt to my mind. It's all right; and I'm bound to say stan'ing here, that con-sidering that Mr. Dugdale guv' up the sea a good bit ago, he's managed oncommonly well down to this here time.'

There was a murmur of assent. I thought I would take advantage of this momentary posture in them of appreciation, perhaps of concession.

'Since you are all before me,' said I, 'two excepted, let me ask you a question. You are aware, of course, that from the very beginning of this business I have regarded your whole scheme as the effect of a madman's dream.'

Lush stared at me with an iron face; Forrest, with an impudent grin, shook his head; two or three of the fellows smiled incredulously. I proceeded, eyeing them deliberately one after the other, and speaking in the most collected tones I could command.

'I want to know this : If Captain Braine's island should have no existence in fact, what do you men propose to do ?'

'No use putting it in that way!' exclaimed the carpenter, after a brief pause, and a slow, sour wagging of his head ; 'the island's there. 'Tain't no dream. Ye'll find it right enough, I'll warrant.'

'It was described to me,' I went on, 'as little more than a reef. This is a big sea, men. A reef is easily missed in such an ocean as this.'

'You have its bearings,' exclaimed Forrest defiantly ; 'if you put the barque in the place on the chart where the captain said the island is, how are we agoing to miss it, unless all hands turns puppies, and keeps a lookout with their eyes shut ? '

' But,' said I, preserving my temper, ' may not this hope of obtaining a large treasure have rendered you all very considerably over-confident ? Suppose there is no island. Reason with me on that supposition. Imagine that we have arrived, and that there is nothing but clear water. Imagine, if you will, that we have been sweeping those seas for a month without heaving into sight your late captain's reef. What then, I ask ? What next steps have you in your minds to take ? I have a right to an answer, even though I should address you only in the name of the young lady whose protector I am.'

The fellows glanced at one another. Their low, suspicious intelligence manifestly witnessed some strategic fancy underlying my question.

' Look here, Mr. Dugdale,' exclaimed the carpenter, ' there's no use in your a-putting it in any other way than the way we want, and the way we mean to have.' He accompanied this with a violent nod of the head. ' Though we're plain men without e'er a stroke of book-learning amongst us, we ain't to be made fools of. The island's where 'ee can find it, if ye choose, and to that there island we're bound, sir;' and he bestowed another emphatic, malevolent nod upon me.

I gazed at the fellows in silence. One glance at the array of mulish countenances should have satisfied me that there was nothing in anything I could say to induce in them other views than those they held, or to render endurable to them a discussion that must be based upon a probability of their being disappointed.

'We've stuck to our side of the bargain, sir,' said one of them.

'Ay,' cried the carpenter; 'I allow that let the gent strive as he may, there's nothen he can find in the treatment him and the lady's met with from us men to complain of.'

'I do not complain,' I exclaimed; 'have you on your side any reason to complain?'

'No, sir, and we don't want none,' the fellow responded with a look that rendered his words indescribably significant.

'You are satisfied, I hope,' said I, 'with the explanation I have given you as to the situation and course of the barque?'

'Yes,' answered the carpenter, with a look round.

'Then there is nothing more to be said,' I exclaimed, and picking up the chart, I carried it into my cabin.

CHAPTER XXXVIII

LAND !

OUR progress was slow. For some while we
carried strong winds, which swept us onwards
into the softer climates of the Pacific ; they
then failed us, and were followed by a succes-
sion of light airs, as often ahead as astern. I
was astonished, however, by the yacht-like
qualities of motion of the little barque.
Through weather that had scarcely weight
enough in it to have stirred the *Countess Ida*,
the *Lady Blanche* would sneak over a surface
of water that was often glass-like, ripples fine
as wire breaking away from her keen stem,
and a short wake scoring the liquid smooth-
ness under her counter : her topsails and
courses motionless, save but for their soft
swaying to the long and gentle respiration of
the swell ; a faint lifting, however, perceptible
in the light cloths of the loftier sails, which
were doing the work of the rest, and com-

municating to the little fabric out of the
delicate softness of the blue Pacific heavens,
so to speak, an impulse of vitality, the recollection of which would move me to amazement
when I found that our progress in the twenty-
four hours had been as considerable as the
Indiaman would have got out of a pleasant
breeze.

But not to linger upon this time—though
I could tell much of my incessant intimate
association with Miss Temple—dwell with
delight, untinctured by recollection of the
miseries and anxieties of this passage, upon
the memory of the soft and lovely nights of
those delicious parallels, the clear dusk radiant
with the glistening of stars from sea-line to
sea-line, the mild atmosphere, sweet with dew,
the hush upon the slumbering leagues of the
deep, soothing as a benediction to the per-
turbed spirit, the play of delicate fires in the
water, the stirring of canvas in the still gloom
aloft, as of the brushing of the pinions of
hovering creatures: then the wide blue sparkling scene of day, the barque clothed in the
ivory whiteness of her canvas striking a pris-
matic shadow of pearl from her white sides
and silken heights into the opalescent pro-

found, on which she would rest as on a bed of glass, some distant fountain and curve of wet black body denoting the rising of a leviathan from the depths—ah! had all been well with us, this would have made a noble time for the memory to muse on—but my story draws me to its conclusion.

It was February the 18th, as very well indeed do I remember. From the hour of our having sighted the whaler off Cape Horn, we had met with nothing, not even of the bigness of the tip of the wing of a sea-fowl, to break the continuity of the sea-line, no shadow of low-lying land, no vision of star-like space of water indicating the froth of the submerged reef. On this day at noon, having worked out my calculations, I discovered that the distance to Braine's island, as I may call it, from the then situation of the barque, was to be traversed, if the light air held as it was, in about twelve hours; so that it would be proper to keep a lookout for it at about midnight.

I gave Mr. Lush this piece of news; he received it with a flush of excitement that almost humanised the insipid coarseness of his dull, wooden, leather-bound, weather-hardened visage.

'Ye may calculate upon our keeping a bright lookout, sir,' said he with a grin that disclosed his tobacco-coloured fangs, and that might fairly be called sardonic, since the eyes bore no part in this disagreeable expression of satisfaction.

I watched him walk forwards to convey the information to the men. They went in a whole body on to the forecastle, and stood staring about them, as though the ocean wore a new countenance to their gaze, now that they believed Braine's island to be a short distance past the slope of it. The carpenter pointed, and was full of talk; there was much lighting of pipes, expectoration, puffing. of great clouds indicative of emotion, uneasy, impatient, flitting movements amongst the men, some of whom presently broke up into couples and fell to pacing the forecastle like marines on sentry; talking, as I did not doubt, of the money they were going to dig up, what they would do with it when they had it, and so on; the expressions on their faces varying at every instant, one emotion suppressing another in a manner that to a contemplative.

and leisurely eye would have provided a study at once ludicrous and informing.

I had the watch that afternoon; and when Miss Temple and I had eaten our little midday meal, I drew chairs into the shadow of the short awning, and we sat together, I, pipe in mouth, occasionally quitting her side to take a look outside the edge of our canvas roof, along with a brief stare ahead, for I could not be sure of Captain Braine's chronometer, nor of the exactness of my own calculations, and if the madman's island was where he had declared it to be, it might heave into view off either bow or right ahead at any moment, for all I could tell.

Miss Temple stood in no need now of Captain Braine's overcoat. She was habited in the costume of the *Countess Ida*; somewhat soiled it was, yet the perfect fit of it continued to atone for its shipwrecked airs. Her dark eyes glowed under the shadow of the straw hat she had had on when she left the Indiaman. She needed but her jewelry, the flash and decoration of her trinkets, to show very nearly as finely as she had on that day. There was but little alteration visible in her. For my part I could detect no more than that her

face was a trifle thinner than when we had
first entered on this wild adventure. The eye
of close and constant association would not
indeed witness changes which might instantly
be perceptible to one encountered after an
absence. Still, I had the image of her brilliant on my mind as she was on board the
Indiaman, and viewing her now, as I say, I
could perceive no other change than what I
have mentioned. Intellectually, however,
there was an alteration, defined to a degree to
my sight. Her gaze was softened, and was
often sweet. The characteristic firmness of
her lips had lost its air of haughtiness. There
was no longer any manner of command in her
looks, nor of exaction in her fixed regard;
there was nothing to hint that her spirit was
broken—merely that it had been bowed to
an average human level by the rough usage
of the sea, and by the amazing experiences
with which her months of lonely association
with me had been surcharged.

Heretofore, that is to say for some weeks
past, she had exhibited a resigned, calm, resolved behaviour, as of one who was constantly schooling herself to prepare for an
issue of life or death. She had long ceased to

utter a complaint; she would even detect a
sigh in herself with a glance of contrition and
self-reproach. Again and again had I complimented her upon the heroic qualities which
her sufferings of mind and body had fructified
in her; but this afternoon she was feverishly
impatient and restless. The old fires of her
spirit when alarmed were in her eyes. I would
observe her struggling in vain to appear composed. As we sat together, she exclaimed,
as she brought her eyes to my face from a
nervous sweeping gaze at the horizon over
the bows: 'By this time to-morrow we shall
know our fate.'

'Perhaps not. Yet I pray it may be so.
If I were sentenced to be hanged, I would
wish the hour come. But what is to be our
fate? Nothing in this life is so bad or so
good as our fears or our hopes would have
us think. If there should be no island——
Well, those villains will find me on the alert
for what may come along in the shape of
chance, and you must be ready.'

'I am ready,' she exclaimed; 'only tell
me what to do. But this expectation——'
Her lips trembled, and her white fingers
clenched to the agitation that possessed her.

'The misery is, Mr. Dugdale, you have no scheme.'

'That will come,' I exclaimed; 'be calm, and remain hopeful. I might, in the language of the heroes of novels, hope to reassure you by promising that if we are to perish we will perish together. I am not a hero, and I talk with the desire and the intention of living. There may be a few more adventures yet before us; but your hand is in mine, and I shall not relinquish it until I conduct you to your mother's side.'

Of course I talked only to cheer her; yet I hoped even as I spoke, and my hope gave a tone of conviction to my words that seemed to animate her, and she smiled whilst her wistful eyes sank, as though to a sudden reverie.

During the rest of the day the crew were ceaselessly on the move, passing in and out of the galley and in and out of the forecastle, pacing the planks with impatience strong in their rolling gait; one or another of them from time to time springing on to the head rail to peer thirstily and steadfastly under the shelter of his hand; one or another again at long intervals ascending to the height of the

foreroyal yard, there to linger, whilst the
fellows below gazed up with expectant faces,
and ears greedy for a cry from that lofty
summit. The sturdy figure of the carpenter
was conspicuous amongst them. When he
came aft, he would look as though willing to
converse with me, but I walked away abruptly
on his approach, and if I chanced to leave
the cabin when he was on deck, I kept to the
lee side, contriving an air that even to his
unintelligent gaze must have conveyed the
assurance that I wished to have nothing to
do with him.

The breeze was light, just forward enough
on the beam to allow of the foretopmast
studding-sail remaining abroad. So weak
was the air, that the barque crept along with
erect spars, and the red fly of the dogvane
scarcely flickered to the soft breathings at the
royal mast head. I feared that it would fall
a dead calm at sun-down, but greatly to my
satisfaction, there was a small freshening in
the breeze whilst the scarlet yet lay gloriously
upon the cloudless countenance of the west.
Indeed, my own almost crazy anxieties and
expectation made the mere fancy of a spell
of stagnation abhorrent to me. Supposing

the chronometer below to be correct, I was
in little doubt of the accuracy of my com-
putations, and my desire to verify or disprove
the madman's assurance was consuming and
insupportable.

When the night descended it was moon-
less, and through the pleasant blowing of the
wind, of a singular sweetness and freshness
such as I could not imagine of darkness in
any other ocean. The water was now streaming in a line of whiteness along either side,
and the murmur under the counter was as
constant as the voice of a running brook
heard amid the stillness of a summer night.
The carpenter had the watch from eight to
twelve : but for my part I could not find it
in me to go to my cabin. Such was my
feverishly restless condition, that I knew I
should close my eyes in vain, and that the
inactivity of a recumbent posture would
speedily grow irksome and intolerable. Miss
Temple entreated me to lie down upon the
locker in the cabin. I answered that I should
be unable to sleep, and that without sleep the
mere resting of my limbs would be of no
service to me.

'But you will have to watch from twelve

to four,' she exclaimed, ' and at this rate you
will get no sleep to-night.'

I smiled, and answered that Braine and
the carpenter between them had murdered
sleep; and then took her on deck, where we
walked and conversed till the hour of eleven
—six bells. I then returned with her to the
cabin. She declined to enter her berth; she
begged me, and her eyes pleaded with her
voice, to suffer her to remain at my side
throughout the night. But this I would not
hear of; I told her that such a vigil would
exhaust her, that her utmost strength might
have to be taxed sooner than either of us
could imagine; that she must endeavour to
obtain some repose upon the locker, and that
if anything resembling land showed during
my watch, I would call her. I saw a look of
reproachful remonstrance in her face; but
compliance was now a habit with her, and in
silence she allowed me to arrange a pillow
and to throw a light blanket, that I fetched
from her bed, over her feet. I sat near her
at the table, leaning my cheek on my elbow,
and from time to time exchanged a few words
with her. There was hardly any movement
in the sea. The wind held the canvas motion-

less. The seething alongside was too delicate
to penetrate, and the silence in the little cuddy
was unbroken save by the ticking of a small
brass clock under the skylight, and by the
measured tramp of the carpenter overhead.

A little before twelve I looked at my companion, and perceived that she was asleep.
On the eve, as I believed we were, of God
alone knew what sort of events, the spectacle of the slumbering unconscious girl, whose
beauty was never so affecting as when softened,
and I may say spiritualised by the expression of placid repose, moved me to the heart.
What a strange association had been ours!
How intimate had we become! what confi-
dences had our common suffering caused us
to exchange! what condition of shoregoing
life was there that could have brought this
girl and me together as we had been and still
were? How I loved her, I was now knowing;
I could dwell upon my passion with delight
as I looked at her, though on the threshold of
a future that might prove terrible and de-
structive to us both. What was the secret of
her heart, so far as I was concerned? I gazed
at her lips with some unintelligible hope of
witnessing them shape the syllables of my

name; then the clear chimes of eight bells floated aft. With a sigh and a prayer, I dimmed the cabin lamp and went softly to the companion steps.

On my emerging, the carpenter came up to me.

'It's been blowing a steady air o' wind,' said he; 'allowing for this here improvement in our pace, what time d'ye reckon the island'll take to show itself?'

'If it exists,' I answered, 'it might be in sight now. The captain's description showed that there was no height of side to make a loom of. If you're going forward, see that a couple of hands are stationed on the forecastle, and tell them to keep a bright lookout. We don't want to run the reef down, if it's there.'

'Ay, ay, sir,' he exclaimed in the rough off-hand voice of a sailor receiving an order, and left the poop.

The time crept away. There was a light burning in the galley; and the shapes that flitted in and out through the open door, throwing giant shadows upon the hazy square of illumination on the bulwark abreast of the galley entrance, satisfied me that most if not

all of the men were awake and on the lookout. Several figures, never less than two,
paced against the stars over the bows with
the regular tread of sentinels, clear on the
forecastle under the forecourse by the spaces
of the spangled sky they blotted out as they
moved. The breeze continued a pleasant
air, and all about the gliding barque were
the summer tinkling sounds of water gently
broken. Occasionally, I would go forward,
and taking my stand on the rise of the cat-
head where it sloped to the rail, strain my
eyes into the elusive starry dusk where sea
and sky seemed to melt into liquid gloom. No
one accosted me as I passed to and fro. Once
I heard the tones of the carpenter in the
galley warm in argument. The fellows pacing
the forecastle would come to a halt whenever
I went forward, and stand looking at me in
silence, full of expectation, no doubt, of my
being able to see more than they. The very
barque herself seemed to participate in the
emotions, the breathless curiosity, the avid
yearnings of the men who awaited the appearance of the island with restless motions and
voices subdued into low growling notes:
the ship herself, I say, seemed governed by

the impassioned expectation of the hour, so tremulously breathless was she aloft, so still and subtle was her movement through the water, so hearkening the aspect of her forward, as though the stirless curve of her jibs were ears which she eagerly projected that she might catch the first sound of the wash of surf.

All this while Miss Temple lay soundly sleeping below.

It was wanting about ten minutes to four when the quarter-deck was suddenly hailed from the forecastle. The voice rang loud and startlingly upon the ear used to the continued stillness of the night.

'Hallo!' I cried.

'There's something dark right ahead,' came back the answer.

I whipped the glass out of the companion, and walked swiftly forwards where all the crew had run to the first cry, and where I found them standing in a huddle of shadowy shapes at the rail, some pointing, and all looking in one direction.

'Where away is the object reported?' I exclaimed.

'Yonder,' cried the carpenter, stepping

out of the little crowd and projecting his arm almost on a line with the jib-boom end.

I instantly perceived it! It was just a streak of shadow, low-lying, like a line of cloud beheld by night lifting a few fathoms of its brow above the sea-line. I pointed the telescope; and the lenses without revealing features, resolved the length of airy obscurity into the firm proportions of land.

'Is it the island, sir?' demanded the carpenter in a voice hoarse with excitement.

My own astonishment—the wonder raised in me by yonder prompt settlement of the incredulity that had possessed me from the first minute of hearing the captain's story—the conflict of emotions which followed on my considering that the land ahead must inevitably be Braine's island, since the chart showed clear water to the distance of the latitude of Easter Island, which the low stretch over the bows most assuredly was not, the loom being little more than that of a reef—rendered my ear deaf to the carpenter's inquiry. He repeated his question.

'If not, then I know not what other land it can be,' said I. 'How far distant will it be, think you?'

The men gathered about us to hear what was said.

'Three mile about,' he answered.

'More like five,' grumbled out a seaman.

'Five in your eye!' cried another—'more like *tew*. If ye'll stay your breathing, you'll hear the wash o' the surf.'

'Better shorten sail and wait for daylight, Mr. Lush,' said I.

'Ay, ay, sir,' he answered; 'that'll be the proper thing to do;' and instantly fell to bellowing out orders.

The uproar of the excited crew clewing up and hauling down, yelling as they pulled at the ropes, and springing about with an alacrity that made their darting figures resemble those of madmen, awakened Miss Temple. I stood alone on the poop, endeavouring to obtain a view of the land by leaning over the rail, when she came up to me.

'What is it, Mr. Dugdale?'

'Land!' I exclaimed, instantly turning to her.

'The island?' she cried, suppressing astonishment until she should have received my answer.

'I have no doubt of it. The shadow in-
dicates that it is little more than a reef. Its
bearings, according to my computation, accurately correspond with those given by Captain
Braine.'

She projected her head over the rail, but
was some time before she could distinguish
the mere dash of gloom that the land made
upo n the horizon.

'If it should be the island!' she cried.
'That you should have steered this ship
straight as an arrow for it, and that it should
be there—no madman's dream, as we have
both believed it! If one part of the story be
true, the other part should be so.'

I was too astounded to converse. I could
do no more than ejaculate. To be sure, as
my companion had said, if the story of the
island was true, the story of the gold might
be equally true. There would be the treasure,
then, for the men to possess themselves of!
And afterwards?

My brains seemed to whirl like a teetotum
in my skull.

Meanwhile, the sailors had reduced sail
till the barque was now under topsails only,
the rest of the canvas hanging from the yards

in the grip of its gear. The carpenter arrived on the poop.

'Mr. Dugdale,' he exclaimed, in a rough, congratulatory voice, 'you've done wonderfully well, sir. By —— ! but I don't think there's e'er a navigator would have struck it true as a hair as ye have. Ye've got no doubts now left, I allow ? ' and I saw his face darken with the wrinkles of the grin that overspread his countenance.

' What's to follow ? ' I demanded, thinking to take advantage of his mood.

' Why, the gold,' he answered, ' the money, sir ; what we've been a-waiting for ; and what I suspects we'll most of us know what to do with when we gits it.'

' And then ? '

' That'll be a matter for consideration,' he answered, drawing off and going to the rail and staring ahead.

' Back the topsail yard and bring the ship to a stand, Mr. Lush,' said I, ' and get a cast of the lead, will you ? '

These orders were immediately obeyed. The lead ran out to the whole scope of line without touching bottom. There was nothing now to be done but to wait for daylight. A whole eternity seemed to pass before the dawn broke. Then to the sifting of the dull gray faintness over the rim of the eastern sea, the land came stealing out, till, to the sudden soaring of the sun into the clear blue sky of the Pacific morning, it flashed out into its full proportions and distinctive features not a mile off our port beam as we then lay with our maintopsail aback.

The crew, neglecting all discipline and shipboard habit, were assembled in a body on the poop; and thus we all stood looking, I a little distance away from them with Miss Temple at my side. It was a small coral island, apparently of the dimensions that Captain Braine had named. To the northward the smooth water brimmed to a long shelf of coral grit, lustrous as snow in the sparkle of the early sunshine. There was a small rise, green with vegetation, in the centre of the island; how far distant, I could not imagine. Almost abreast of us, the land went in with a semicircular sweep like to a horseshoe, and was exactly the lagoon that had been described by Captain Braine. In the centre of it, just as he had marked the thing down upon his chart, rose a coral formation of the appearance of a very thick pillar, and at the distance from which we surveyed it, it might easily have passed for a monument of white stone erected by human hands, the decorated summit of which had been rudely broken off by a tempest or some volcanic shock. On a line with this pillar, some little distance up the beach of the lagoon, were several clumps of trees. There was a deal of a sort of stunted vegetation going inland from the margin of the little bay, coarse grass, as my telescope made out, tangles of bushes, and so on.

The carpenter in the midst of the men stood with the parchment chart in his hand, pointing out how the outlines corresponded with those of the land, amidst a hubbub of eager comments and exclamations of excitement. For my part, I could not credit my senses; I disputed the evidence of my own eyes; I brought them away from the island to fix them with an emotion of profound bewilderment upon Miss Temple.

'Can it be real?' I cried. 'After the weeks of conviction of the utter madness of this quest, am I at last to be persuaded that the wretched suicide was not mad, that his

island is a fact, and his gold an absolute
reality too ? '

I turned my back upon the crew to press
my hands to my eyes to ease my brow of an
intolerable sense of swooning in it.

' Three cheers for him, men ! ' I heard the
carpenter roar out. Volley after volley of
huzzas rang from the deep sea lungs of the
sailors. They were cheering me. I turned
to find them all looking my way. They tossed
their caps and flourished their arms like madmen in the exuberance of their delight.

'Now, sir,' sung out the carpenter, 'hadn't
we better see to our ground tackle ? '

' As you will,' I answered ; ' there is your
island ; I have kept my word with you ; now,
Mr. Lush, the crew will proceed as they think
proper. When you require my services again
as a navigator I am ready ;' and so saying I
seated myself on the edge of the skylight, and
with folded arms continued to view the island
with such astonishment and incredulity as
made me fear for my head.

' Is it all for the best, do you think, Mr.
Dugdale? ' said Miss Temple, who had seated
herself beside me.

' I cannot tell—it may be so. If they find

the money, the wretches' delight and good
temper may render them willing to comply
with my wishes to make for the nearest port.
I am in a dream. Give me a little time to
recover my amazement. You know it ought
to be impossible that that island should be
there.'

She glanced at me anxiously, with something of alarm indeed, as though there was
even a greater strangeness in my manner than
in my language. Long hours of anxiety, long
hours of sleeplessness, the continual apprehension of what was to follow if this island
was not discoverable, these things and how
much more had done their work with me ;
and now on top was come the shock of the
discovery of the truth of what I had all along
been convinced was the dream of a madman
—the lie of a crazy head ! I felt a moisture
in my eyes ; my limbs trembled ; my breathing
grew thick and difficult. In silence, Miss
Temple hurried below and returned with a
tumbler of cold brandy grog. She put it into
my hand, and I drank it off; and I have very
little doubt that the strong stimulant—such a
dose as might have made me boozy in an hour

of ease !—rescued me from an attack of hysterics, man as I am who tell this !

Meanwhile the seamen had gone forward, and were all hard at work with the chain cables, connecting them with the anchors, affixing tackles, hoisting the ponderous irons to the catheads, and filling the barque with business and songs. They worked with desperate will and eagerness, yet their progress was slow, and the sun had mounted many degrees before all was ready forward for bringing up. They then went tumultuously to breakfast, which they devoured upon deck, emptying their hook-pots down their throats, and hastily eating their biscuit and meat, whilst they jabbered away in voices of enthusiasm, one calling out a joke to another amidst loud laughter.

The carpenter had now taken command. He came aft while Miss Temple and I nibbled at some breakfast which Wilkins had brought us on deck, and ordered the maintopsail to be swung, and stationed a hand with a lead-line in each of the main-chains. The wind was about south, and allowed the barque with her yards braced fore and aft to very nearly look up for the lagoon. We crept slowly along ;

the lead on either hand went in frequent flights towards the bow, but no bottom was reported. This went on till the yawn of the lagoon was upon our starboard quarter, with the trend of the land covered with bushes opening out as it ran into the south-east, and then came a shout from the port main chains. The water now shoaled rapidly ; a man stood forward ready to let go the anchor ; down thundered the topsail yards to the cry of the carpenter to let go the halliards ; the barque lost way; the sharp clank of a hammer rang through the vessel, followed by a mighty splash, and the roar of iron links torn in fury through the hawse-pipes.

In a few moments the *Lady Blanche* was at rest, with the western spur of the lagoon within half a mile of her

CHAPTER XXXIX

THE ISLAND

THE men now went to work to get tackles on
to the yards, in order to hoist the long-boat
over. This again ran into time, for the boat
stood in chocks, and was stoutly lashed to the
deck ; and before they could remove her,
they had to clear away the spare booms which
were stowed on top of her and clean her out.
When they had her alongside, they passed
water and provisions and several gallons of
rum into her, with other matters of this sort,
of which I hardly took notice. They also
handed down the shovels used for the little
stock of coal that was carried in the fore-peak,
and several crows, handspikes, and whatever
else they could lay their hands upon that
would enable many of them at a time to dig
up the soil.

Whilst all this was doing, I remained
seated on the poop with Miss Temple. I was

now feeling better and stronger again, could think rationally, and astonishment was worn out.

'It is most unmistakably the island that Captain Braine named,' I said to the girl, speaking with my eye at the telescope. 'I remember he spoke of a clump of trees at the foot of which the treasure lies hidden. Yonder are several clumps. Which one of them will it be, I wonder? and will the money be there? What an astonishing romance will it prove, should those sailors fall in with a booty of nearly two hundred thousand pounds!'

'What are they going to do, do you think, Mr. Dugdale?'

'It looks to me as if the whole body of them were going ashore to dig.'

'Are they not taking a deal of provisions with them?'

'They may mean to make merry. After months of shipboard life, the touch of the land will be grateful to the soles of their feet. Let them find the gold! their transports will know no bounds; there will be some wild skylarking amongst them before they come off, or I am greatly mistaken. Would to God

they would make themselves drunk, that I
might run away with the ship.'

'Cannot that be done when they are on
shore?' she cried with an air of exultant
entreaty in her sudden leaning towards me as
she spoke.

'Yes, were an off-shore gale to come on
to blow, I might contrive to slip and let the
barque storm out to sea before it. But in
this weather! They would be after me in a
jiffy in their boat, and then God help me
when they got hold of me!'

A shade of paleness overspread her face,
and she regarded me with a look of consternation, as though violently affected by the fancies
my simple sentence had put before her. I
sprang on the top of the hencoop to sweep
the sea-line with the telescope, but could
nowhere discern the least shadow of land.
As I put down the glass, the carpenter came
off the quarter-deck, where, at the gangway,
he had been busily shouting out instructions
and overseeing the work of preparing the
boat, and approached me. He held Captain
Braine's parchment chart, at which he stopped
to look for·a moment when he was yet some
paces distant.

'Will ye tell me what's your opinion of the weather, sir ?' he exclaimed, in a voice whose natural gruffness and surliness were not to be sweetened by the satisfaction that was merely visible in a small symptom of respectfulness in his bearing.

'I do not know, I am sure. This cloudless sky should be full of promise. The mercury in the captain's cabin promises fair weather.'

'What do 'ee think of letting them sails hang ?' said he, sending his malevolent gaze aloft ; ' or shall we tarn to and roll 'em up afore we go ashore ?—though it'll be a long job,' he added, directing his eyes thirstily at the island.

'The ship is in your hands,' said I.

'Oh well,' he exclaimed, as though gratified by my admission, and sending a slow look round the sea ; ' we'll let 'em be as they are for the present. The anchor's got a good grip, I allow ; if so be as a breeze should come along, we can send some of the men aboard to furl the sails.'

We! thought I, as I regarded him in silence.

'My sight ain't what it used to be,' he continued ; ' yet I can see enough of that there island'—and here he began to fumble with the chart he held—'to guess that this here's a first-rate likeness of it. This,' said he, pointing with his square thumb at the mark in the middle of the lagoon on the parchment, 'is one of the bearings we've got to have in mind to find out where we're to begin to dig, ain't it?'

'I believe so,' said I.

'Didn't ye put down the particulars of the spot in writing?' he inquired, looking up at me from the chart.

'No,' I answered shortly.

'How many feet was the money hid away from the wash of the water?' he demanded.

'It was in paces, I remember,' I returned, 'but the figure is entirely gone out of my head. Wilkins should be able to recollect.'

He ran with a sort of dismay to the break of the poop and bawled for Wilkins. The lad came half-way up the steps. The carpenter spoke to him and then returned.

'The young scowbanker don't recall,' he exclaimed. 'He believes—a curse on his believes!—that the captain spoke of four hundred feet. Was that it, sir?'

'I remember enough to make sure that it was not four hundred feet,' I answered.

He picked up the glass and levelled it at the island.

'Which of them clumps of trees was it that the capt'n talked to ye about?' he asked whilst he looked.

'He did not describe any particular clump. It was to be found by measuring so many paces from the edge of the water of the lagoon yonder, the pillar bearing something west, but what I can't tell you. I treated the story as a madman's dream, and dismissed all the particulars of it from my mind.'

'We'll have to try all them clumps, then, that's all,' said he, with a hard face and a voice at once sharp and coarse with ill-subdued temper. 'We'll get the money, though it comes to having to dig up the whole island. And now, sir, there's nothen to stop us—the boat's ready—if you'll be pleased to come along.'

'I can be of no good to you,' I exclaimed with an involuntary recoil; 'you have hands enough to dig. I'll stop here.'

'No, if you please; we shall want you,'

he said, with a stare of dogged determination.

'I must not be left alone, Mr. Lush,' cried Miss Temple, with a painful expression of fear in her bloodless face. 'If Mr. Dugdale goes, I must accompany him.'

'No, mem. You're safe enough here. We must have Mr. Dugdale along with us to show us what to do. For Lord's sake, no arguments, sir! The impatience of the men 'll be forcing them to taking you up in their arms and lifting you over the side, if you keep 'em waiting.'

'But am I to understand,' I exclaimed, 'that all hands of you intend to quit the ship, leaving this lady alone on board?'

'Joe Wetherly and Jim Simpson 'll remain, he replied; 'they'll keep a lookout, and two's enough with us men in hail of their voices. Now, sir, if you please.'

The crew standing in the gangway were looking my way with signs of irritation in their bearing. I merely needed to give one glance at the carpenter's face to satisfy me that temper, protest, appeal, would be hopeless; that refusal must simply end in my being bodily laid hold of. I was urged by every instinct in me to a policy of conciliation. To irritate the fellows would be the height of folly; to provoke the indignity of being seized and roughly thrust into the boat, the utmost degree of madness. My resolution was at once formed.

'I will accompany you, Mr. Lush,' I said. 'Get you gone on to the quarter-deck whilst I say a few words to comfort my companion.'

He walked away to the gesture with which I accompanied this request.

'Miss Temple, pray take heart. Wetherly is one of the two men who are to be left. You will feel safe here with him on board until I return.'

'Until you return!' she cried, with her eyes full of misery and horror. 'I shall never see you more!'

'Oh no; do not believe such a thing. The men imagine I shall be of service to them in lighting upon the spot where the gold is. They cannot do without me as a navigator. They will bring me off with them when they leave the island.'

'I shall never see you again,' she repeated in a voice of exquisite distress. 'Why could they not have left us together here?'

' Now, Mr. Dugdale, if *you* please,' bawled the carpenter from the head of the poop ladder.

I took and pressed her hand between mine, and then broke away from her. What had I to say, what to offer, that she could convert into a hope? I felt the danger of continuing to view her in her despair and helplessness, for already it was producing in me a rage against the men that must be suppressed at all costs. I turned to smile and to wave my hand, and found her with her back upon me and her face buried.

Wetherly and the man who was to be left with him stood a little forward of the main-hatch looking on. As I stepped to the gangway I called out : ' Wetherly, and you, Simpson : I leave the lady behind me ; she is alone. You will see to her, men, I beg.'

Simpson gazed stolidly, as though not understanding me ; indeed, there was no countenance amongst the sailors from which all meaning appeared to have been so entirely discharged as his. Wetherly smiled, and flourished his hand with a significant glance. He would perfectly comprehend that I had

included Simpson as an excuse to appeal to
him only. Without another word I dropped
into the main-chains and jumped into the
long-boat.

When the men had entered, there were
ten of us in all. The boat was a roomy,
stoutly-built fabric, and her oars were almost
as long as sweeps. The barque's quarter-boats
would have been too small for this service;
for the ten of us made a body, and they had
handsomely stowed her besides with water
and rum and provisions (as you are aware),
not to mention the sundries with which they
proposed to dig the soil. I rather wondered
that they should have supplied themselves so
hospitably, till I recollected that Captain
Braine had said there was no fresh water and
nothing to eat upon the island. The carpenter
had no doubt remembered this as a passage
in the story which Wilkins had overheard and
repeated. It might be also that they intended
to stay awhile on this island when they had
dug up the gold, to refresh themselves, with
the substantiality of land under their feet, for
a day or two after their long months of the
heaving sea; in which case they would natu-
rally convey what they required at once, to

spare themselves the trouble of a trip to the ship.

Their leaving Wetherly behind was due, I took it, to the indifference and doubt he had exhibited from the commencement ; possibly, they might also have some notion, by requiring him to remain on board, to cheat him of a portion of his share ; and since they considered that two were necessary to watch the barque, they would find a willingness to remain in her only in the stupidest man amongst them, who, to be sure, was Simpson. These were thoughts which hurriedly passed through my mind even whilst the fellows were in the act of shoving off. There was neither sail nor mast in the boat. Probably they considered that those things would encumber the thwarts, whilst, in fact, there was no real need for them, since the vessel lay within a very easy pull. Four fellows threw their oars over, and the boat clumsily broke the smooth water to the impulse of their blades.

When we were clear of the shadow of the barque's side, I turned to look for Miss Temple, and observed her seated in a posture of utter despondency upon the skylight. I stood up and flourished my hat; but she made no

sort of response. She remained motionless,
as though stupefied and insensible. I resumed
my seat, breathing hard with the wild mood
that possessed me; but I was not to be suffered
to sit in silence. The carpenter plied me with
questions, which he only ceased that the
others might have a chance of making inquiries. Couldn't I remember how many
paces it was that the captain had said? Would
it be one hundred? Would it be two hundred? Would I turn to and think a bit?
A gent's eddicated memory was always better
than plain men's, who weren't no scholards.
If the right number of paces wasn't hit upon,
it might take 'em a week to find the spot.
And what about the bearings? Couldn't I
recollect exactly how the trees bore from
that there pillar? Wherever the gold was,
it couldn't lie deep hid, for there was but two
men to bury it, and them weak with shipwreck, and they wasn't going all the way
down to hell to make sartin of a secret nook.

To all this I had to listen and reply as 1
best could. Yet it was talk to put a fancy
that had long haunted me—that had haunted
me, I may say, from the time of some of my
earliest conversations with the carpenter—

into shape, out of which arose one instantly present keen perception : that gold or no gold, they must be kept hunting for it !

It was a cloudless day ; the sky a true Pacific blue, a mild breathing of wind off the island ; and the sun, that was already at his meridian, flung a wide splendour upon the air that was without an insufferable excess of heat. The long-boat floated into the lagoon, the bottom of which showed like a pavement of white marble trembling through the blue, glass-like translucency. I looked carefully about me, but could see no signs of the hut which Captain Braine told me he had built, and out of which he had crawled to find the Yankee surveying craft hove-to abreast of the island. Neither were there any other relics of his shipwreck visible : such as the bottles, casks, tins, and so on, which, according to his account, he and his companion had landed from the brigantine. It is true that a good many years had elapsed since the date of the wreck as he had given it me, and in that time the island might have been visited or swept by seas and hurricanes. The sailors did not appear to heed the absence of all memorials of Captain Braine's having landed here.

'The Spanish craft'll have come ashore yonder,' said the carpenter, standing erect, referring to Braine's story, and indicating by an eager nod of the head the position of the stretch of lustrous beach that looked northwards, but that was now invisible to us. 'Where'll be a good place to land here?'

All hands were staring about them. The fellow named Forrest said : 'There's a bit of a tree there that'll hold the boat secure. Better let her lay afloat, Mr. Lush, 'case of a change o' weather and having to shove off in a hurry.'

'Ay, she'll lie all right off that tree,' exclaimed the carpenter. 'In oars, lads! Let her slide quietly stem on. I've heard of coral spikes a-tearing of boats' bottoms out.'

A few minutes later most of us were ashore, the boat lying quietly secured by a line to a small but solidly rooted tree, and two or three fellows in her handing out her freight of odds and ends to the others.

The feel of solid land under my feet was a singular sensation. I had now been incessantly at sea for a time that was growing rapidly into six months, and after those interminable weeks of heaving shipboard, the im-

movability of this coral rock affected me as
something in the greatest degree novel. I sent
a hurried glance around ; but the eyes I had
strained from over the rail of the barque had
acquainted me with every material point of
the island, and this closer survey yielded
nothing fresh. The margin of the beach of
the lagoon went gently sloping up from hard
coral to a species of soil that appeared to
possess some qualities of fertility, for the tall
coarse grass was very plentiful and of a most
vivid green. The few groups of trees were
also richly clad, and the bushes extraordinarily abundant. There were no signs of life
of any sort saving birds, of which a score
or two were wheeling about in the air over
the northward fronting beach. The inland
rise was a mere small green acclivity probably
not above thirty feet to the summit. All was
silent, desolate, lifeless ; nothing to hear amid
the brief intervals of stillness among the
men save the delicate noise of the soft
wind amongst the foliage, and the melancholy
moaning of surf from the other side of the
island.

Everything was landed ; the men seized
hold of the various implements they had

brought with them to dig up the soil; the carpenter flourished a shovel and called to me: 'Mr. Dugdale, have ye no recollection of the number of paces?'

'None whatever,' I responded.

'What d'ye advise, sir?'

'Measure a hundred paces, keeping yonder pillar on a line with that clump of trees there, and then dig.'

'Ay, but Wilkins overheard the capt'n say that the money was buried at the foot of some trees,' said Forrest. 'A hundred paces ain't going to bring us near a tree.'

'I remember nothing about the foot of some trees,' I exclaimed.

'What do *you* recall?' the carpenter shouted to Wilkins.

'I thought I heerd something about the foot of trees,' answered the fellow, turning his pale meaningless countenance upon Lush. But Mr. Dugdale'll know best, of course.'

'If the money be here at all,' said I, 'you may take it as lying hidden somewhere in this space,' and with pointing finger I indicated an oblong surface one end of which went a little beyond the fourth group of trees, whilst I defined the other as starting from about a hundred paces away from the edge of the beach where the boat was.

Ten minutes were now expended in heated discussion. Where should they begin? One or two were for leaving it to me and carrying out my suggestions; others were for measuring two hundred paces and starting there; whilst others were for digging at the roots of the clumps of trees, taking them one after another.

'See here, lads,' cried the carpenter; 'we han't had anything to eat yet. Better tarn to and get some dinner and grog. By that time we shall ha' settled what to do and be the fitter to go to work.'

This was a proposal which all hands found perfectly agreeable. They flung down the implements they held, and in a very short time were seated about the grass, sheath-knives in hand, making a hearty meal off salt beef and biscuit and cheese, and tossing down pannikins of rum-and-water. They invited me to join them, and treated me with all the respect I could desire. Again and again, whilst we thus sat, I would direct looks at the barque as she lay as it might seem almost within musket-shot of us. The figure of a man paced the forecastle; but Miss Temple was not to be seen. Once the carpenter, catching me looking, exclaimed with a sort of enthusiasm in his voice : 'Well, the little hooker *is* a beauty and no mistake. What a slaver she'd make!' Commendation probably could not go higher in such a man. A beauty, indeed, she looked; the reflection of her white sides floated under her like a wavering sheet of silver; her canvas hanging in festoons showed with the milk-white softness of streaks of clouds against the blue sky past her; her rigging had the exquisite minuteness of hair. Would to God, I thought to myself with a sudden heavy sinking of my heart, that I were on board of her alone with Miss Temple, ay, with no other hands than mine to work the ship! I should find the strength of half-a-dozen seamen in me for her sake. Poor girl! and there arose before me a vision of the Indiaman—a recollection of the proud Miss Temple scarcely enduring to send a glance my way—— But this was a reverie that must be speedily disturbed by the company I was in.

They had hoarsely debated until they had come to an agreement, and, having concluded

their meal, each man lighted his inch of
sooty clay, picked up his shovel or his crow,
or whatever else had been brought off from
the barque, and marched to the nearest of
the clump of trees, at the foot of which they
fell to digging. Every man was in motion ;
they laboured with incredible activity, and
with such faces of rapturous expectation as
again and again forced a smile from me,
depressed, anxious, miserable as I was. With
my hands clasped behind me, I paced to and
fro, watching and waiting. Now that the
island had proved an absolute fact, I could
no longer feel certain that the gold was a madman's fancy. Nay, I was now indeed imagining that it was all true, and that Braine had
fallen crazy through possession of his incom-
municable secret acting upon a mind congeni-
tally tinctured with insanity, and irremediably
weakened yet by the horrible sufferings he
had undergone before he was cast away upon
this spot. Yet never did I glance at the
barque without a prayer trembling from my
heart to my lips that the wretches might not
find the gold. An old scheme, that this
unexpected lighting upon the island had
quickened and given shape to, was fast

maturing in my mind, even while I paced
that stretch of grass; but the discovery of
the money would render it abortive.

I watched the seamen with an interest as
keen as their own, but with hopes diametri-
cally opposite. The soil was dry, stubborn,
perhaps through the intermingling of coral-
grit and the coarse fibres of its herbage. Yet
there were many of them, and every man
worked with desperate energy, and presently
they had dug up a good space to some little
depth. I awaited with a beating heart the
exultant shout which I might be sure the first
man who turned up one of the yellow pieces
would raise. They continued to toil in
silence. Presently the carpenter, resting his
chest upon his shovel, with the sweat falling
in rain from his crimson face, bawled out to
me: ' How fur down, d'ye think, we ought to
keep on a-digging?'

' I would give up at two feet,' said I.
' Captain Braine and his friend would not
find strength to go much beyond two feet.'

One of the fellows plumbed with his crow,
and, bringing it out, with his thumb at the
height of the level, cried: ' It's more'n two
feet already.'

They dug a little longer, nevertheless; then a few curses ran among them, and the carpenter, with a note of irritation in his voice, roared out : 'No good going on here. Try this clump.' He walked over to it and drove his shovel into the soil. The men gathered about him, and in a trice were all in motion again.

This was a severity of toil that I knew must force them to break off presently. Although I could not distinctly recollect the bearings of the treasure as given by Captain Braine, I felt persuaded that he had named the base of the group of trees which the fellows had just quitted as the hiding-place of the money. If it were not there, then I might feel perfectly satisfied it was nowhere else, and hope began to dawn in me afresh. Their labour at the base of the second clump resulted in nothing. They exposed a wide space, and went deep, but to no purpose. The time had passed rapidly; I looked at my watch, and was astonished to find it hard upon five o'clock.

All this while the sky had remained cloudless, and there was no hint visible in any part of its countenance of a change in this

softness and tranquillity of weather. The
light off-shore draught, however, had shifted
into the west, and at this hour there was a
cool and pleasant breeze, that brushed the
breast of the sea into a surface of twinkling
ripples. The water of the lagoon trembled
to it as it breathed laterally athwart its face,
and already the coral beach of this graceful
wide-mouthed inlet bore on the lee-side its
stress of tiny breakers.

The sailors by this time were pretty well
exhausted. The expressions their faces wore,
so far as they might be determinable amid
the purple, and perspiration, and hair of their
dripping and fire-hot visages, showed them
full of irritability and disappointment. The
carpenter addressed them ; I did not catch
what he said, but as they came in a body
towards the part of the beach where I had
been pacing or sitting whilst they worked, I
could hear them swearing and cursing, whilst
they grumbled and growled out their sur-
mises as to where the money was hidden,
their eyes roving over the soil as they talked.
Lush's face was hard with temper.

'We're agoing to send off some men to
furl the lighter canvas,' said he. 'Ha'n't got

much opinion of this soil as holding-ground,
and she'll drag with that weight of canvas
loose, and blow away out of soundings, if we
don't see to it.'

'A very proper precaution,' said I coolly.
'You don't mean to give up digging yet, I
suppose?'

'Give up?' he cried with his coarse sarcastic air, and frowning upon me out of the
rage my inquiry excited. 'No; not if we
has to dig the whole island up, as I told ye.'

'Very well. I'll go aboard with the men
in the boat. The money, if it is hidden at
all, will be hereabouts,' said I, with a wave
of my arm, 'and I can be of no further use
to you.'

'No, no; you'll stop along with us, if you
please,' said the fellow. 'Your recollection
of the number of paces may come back to ye,
and we can't do without you.'

I sent a look from him to the faces of the
fellows who stood listening near us, and without another word folded my arms, and with
a spin of my heel started off on a walk to and
fro.

CHAPTER XL

I ESCAPE

If I had witnessed the idleness of protest and remonstrance and appeal on board the barque, I must have held entreaty to be tenfold more useless in the face of the mortification of the carpenter and his crew, increased as their temper was by the irritation and the fatigue of hard and useless work. I might at once be sure that they had no intention of suffering me to leave the island until they quitted it themselves for good. There would be also distrust; the fear that I might contrive to run away with the ship. Yet I had still to find out what they meant to do; what their plans were for the night. I knew what I wanted, and I remember what I prayed for as I tramped solitarily backwards and forwards upon the edge of the herbage where it came thin to the beach.

Seven men entered the long-boat and

shoved off. The carpenter remained; with him was the sailor named Woodward. They flung themselves down upon the ground with an air of exhaustion, and so lay smoking their pipes. After awhile, the carpenter called to me. I approached him leisurely. He asked me if I remembered the number of paces from the beach, and eyed me so surlily as he put the inquiry that I began to think he suspected I could tell if I chose.

'If Wilkins can't remember,' I exclaimed, 'why should I be able to do so—I, whose opinion of this business you well know? I do not recollect the number of paces. I wish I did, for I am more anxious than ever you can be that you should come at this gold, that we may sail away, and end the most cursed adventure that ever a man was forced into.'

The heat and the evident sincerity with which I spoke these words slightly subdued him, and his ugly face relaxed its threatening look. Finding him silent I said: 'What do you mean to do?'

'Stop here all night,' he answered shortly. 'Stop here, I've told ye, till we've found the money.'

'You will leave some men aboard the ship to look after her?'

'Two'll be quite enough,' he answered. 'How much looking after do she want in weather of this pattern? If we don't meet with the gold afore dark—and there'll be no chance of *that*, I allow—we must all be at hand to tarn to at daybreak.'

I asked no further questions; and the fellow sank into silence, both he and the other sucking at their pipes, whilst they seemed to hunt with their eyes over the ground as they lay with their heads propped on their elbows.

I saw Miss Temple on the poop watching the approaching boat. Very well could I imagine the feeling which would possess her when she perceived that I was not among the occupants of the little craft! The boat clumsily drove alongside, and the men sprang on board over a short rope gangway ladder that had been dropped. They went to work at once, as though in a hurry to get the furling job over, that they might return; and with a swiftness that was surprising in fellows almost exhausted by previous labour, they furled the mainsail, foresail, and lighter canvas, leaving the topsails hanging, and the spanker loosely·brailed in to the mast. This done, they descended, and came to a pause at the gangway, as though giving what news they had to the two seamen that had been left behind. They then entered the boat afresh and leisurely made for the island. As they jumped on to the beach, I noticed that the man Simpson had taken the place of Forrest, who had been left to keep a lookout with Wetherly. I felt instantly very uneasy on observing this. There was no other man of all the crew whom 1 would not sooner have wished to be Wetherly's associate than that impudent, mutinous, bold-faced young seaman. To think of Miss Temple alone with those two men! one to be trusted, as I hoped and believed; but the other as insolent and defiant a rascal as could be imagined of any forecastle blackguardly hand! I gazed eagerly at the barque, and was glad to find that the girl had gone below. I earnestly prayed that she would have the sense to keep in hiding. There was the long night before her, and Wetherly might·sleep.

Never since the hour of our losing sight of the Indiaman had I felt half so worried, half so distracted with fears and forebodings.

I withdrew to a distance from that part of the beach where I had been walking, that the workings of my mind might not be seen in my face; and thankful was I afterwards, when I had somewhat cooled down, that the carpenter did not offer to approach or speak to me; for such was the passion my anxiety for Miss Temple had raised, that I believe a single syllable of rudeness would have caused me to fall upon him—with what result it would be useless here to imagine.

There was about an hour and a half of daylight remaining. When the sailors had secured their boat, they went to supper. In lieu of tea they drank rum-and-water, and this pretty plentifully.

'Won't ye jine us, Mr. Dugdale?' called out the carpenter. 'No call to eat along with us if you object to our company. Ye can have your food separate; but you'll be wanting to eat anyhow.'

'He must be a poor sailor who is not good enough company for me,' I exclaimed, having by this time mastered myself; and forthwith I took my seat amongst them and fell to upon a piece of salt beef, whilst I got a stronger

beat for my pulse out of the pannikin of grog
that I drained.

The men's talk was all about the gold.
'If it ain't under them trees,' said one of them,
'it'll ha' to come to doing what the gent told
us; starting at a hundred paces from the wash
of the water there and digging in a line till
we strikes it.'

'What'll them as hid it have wrapped it
up in?' exclaimed another.

'Canvas,' answered the carpenter shortly.

'Which'll have rotted by this time, I
allow, and the money'll be lying loose,' said a
sailor.

'Who'll get the first chink of it?' cried
Wilkins.

Exclamations of this sort I observed
worked a general sense of elation in them;
and the rum helping their spirits, they began
to crack jokes, and their laughter was loud
and frequent. The scene, to any one who
could have viewed it without distress, must
have been thought admirable for its character
of soft romantic beauty. The western atmosphere was brimful of the reddening light of
the descending sun; under it, the smooth
ocean lay in dark gold that came sifting out

into a cool azure, which then ran with an ever-deepening tint of blue into the clear liquid distance. The trembling of the sea to the breeze put a weak coming and going of light and shadow into these dyes, and freshened the western light upon the surface into a very glorious scintillation. The barque floated like a shape of marble in the cerulean water that lay betwixt the reflection of the sun and the darker tints of the east. Her rigging resembled wires of gold, her masthead vane lay like a little flame against the sky, her white shadow fluctuated in dissolving quicksilver under her, and as she slightly leaned with the delicate heave of that wide Pacific breast, stars of crimson flashed off her deck, and her bright lower-masts showed as though they were on fire. The water in the lagoon floated in a tender blue to the coral beach on which it rippled. There was a subtle aroma as of sweet and secret inland vegetation upon the atmosphere. The long grass stirred, and the silken brushing of the leaves of the trees against one another produced the most refreshing sound that could be imagined to ears which for months had received no pleasanter noises than the straining of timbers, the flapping of sails, and the sobbing and washing of the ocean surge. There was nothing in the wildness and rugged looks of the fiery-faced recumbent seamen to impair the tenderness of this picture. On the contrary, their roughness seemed to accentuate its gentle beauty, as the silence of a calm midnight at sea may be heightened by some gruff human voice speaking at a distance, or by some rude sound that assists the hearing as a contrast.

The carpenter looked towards the sun.

'Don't let's waste no more time,' he cried ; 'let's attack that third clump there afore it falls dark.'

They sprang to their feet, seized their several tools, and in a few moments were hard at it, digging, boring, but in silence, for their efforts were too heavy for talk or for laughter. The sun went down whilst they were still toiling. They had discovered nothing, and the first to give up was the carpenter. He sent his shovel flying through the air with a loud curse.

'I'm done for to-night,' he roared. 'Where did them scowbankers hide it ? It'll have to be as Mr. Dugdale says. 'Morrow marning

we'll start at a hundred paces from the beach.
We're not here to miss it, and we'll have it if
we rip the guts of this island out of her forty
fathom deep !'

He was furious with temper and exhaustion, and stepping to a kettle that was full of
rum and water, he half-filled a hook-pot and
swallowed the contents to the dregs, afterwards pitching the vessel from him with an
air of loathing and passion.   The men, throwing their implements into a heap, came slowly
to where the rum and provisions were, cursing
very freely indeed, some of them groaning
with weariness, smearing the sweat off their
foreheads along their naked arms, and stretch-
ing their clenched fists above their heads in
postures of yawning.   Every man of them
took a long drink, and then they slowly fell
to filling their pipes whilst they continued to
heap curses upon Captain Braine and his
companion for not having buried the money
in a place where it might be easily got at.

My heart was now beating quickly with
anxiety.   What was the next step they meant
to take?   Would the carpenter change his
mind and carry all hands of us aboard?   I
observed him light his pipe, and take a look

around with as evil an expression on his face as ever I had witnessed in it. He then trudged with a deep sea-roll in his walk down to the tree to which the boat was attached, and having carefully examined the knot, as though to make sure that the line was securely fastened, he stood gazing awhile at the little craft, as though considering, afterwards sending his eyes in another rolling stare round the horizon as far as it lay visible. I watched him furtively, but with consuming anxiety.

' Tell ye what, mates,' he suddenly sung out, rounding upon the men and approaching them, ' there's nothen to hurt in this weather, and the barque's going to lie as quiet as if she was laid up. We'll just stop where we are ; but a lookout 'll ha' to be kept, and the boat must be watched. Better settle the order at once. The lookout will sit in the boat, case'—he added with a sarcastic leer in my direction—' there might be savages about unbeknown to us with a settlement aback of that hill amidships there. What d'ye say, Mr. Dugdale ? '

' I have no longer command,' I answered ; ' it is for you to arrange as you will. Why you desire to keep me here, I cannot imagine.

Why not put me aboard, that the young lady may have the comfort of my presence ? '

' She don't want no comfort,' he answered coarsely ; ' she's all right. The number of paces the capt'n talked of may come to ye by daybreak, and we're all at hand to tarn to.'

I made no answer.

The night came down dark and clear, with a noise of rippling waters in the quiet steady wind. The barque faded into a phantasm, and inland it was all black as ink, with the stars which rimmed the outline of the central rise winking there like sentinel beacons burning upon some giant mountain leagues distant. But where the boat lay the space of coral grit showed pallid, of the hue of ordinary soil bathed in moonlight, and the figure of the little fabric, with her nose pointing at the tree to which the rope that secured her was fastened, blended shadowily with the darkling surface of the water of the lagoon, over whose tiny ripples the clear reflection of the larger stars were riding.

The men roamed about in twos and threes, but never very far. I believed I could trace an uneasiness in their behaviour, as though they had consented to sleep out of the ship in obedience only to the carpenter's wishes, and were now reconsidering their acquiescence with some indecision of mind. I earnestly hoped that this might not prove so, and watched and listened to them with my heart full of wretchedness. The carpenter was seated with another man, and conversed with him in low notes, which trembled to my ears like the subdued growling of a dog. I strolled away to a distance, but was neither followed nor called to.

The time passed very slowly. The men grew weary of moving about, though for some while the mere sensation of the hard soil was a delight to them, now that the air was deliciously cool and they had no work to do and could roam at will. They came in a body together and seated themselves round about the carpenter and his companion, drinking by the starlight, with the frequent glare of the lighting of pipes throwing out the adjacent faces, till it was like looking into a camera obscura. They talked much, but my attentive ear detected a drowsy note stealing into the sound of grumbling that stood for their conversation.

It was drawing on to the half-hour past

ten when I stepped leisurely up to the huddle
of shadows, and looking over them as they
lay in all sorts of postures, I exclaimed:
'Which is the carpenter?'

'Here he is,' answered the voice of Lush.

'Are the men going to make a bedroom
of this spot?' said I.

'Ay,' he answered. 'Where else? Ye
han't surely come across a hotel in your
lonely rambles?'

These words he pronounced without intending offence, though such was the coarseness of the ruffian that he could say little
which was not offensive. One or two of the
fellows laughed.

'I shall look out for comfortable quarters
for myself,' said I. 'I have no fancy for lying
amidst all this high grass. There may be
snakes about.'

'No, no!' exclaimed one of the men;
'there's no snakes here, sir. I've kept a bright
lookout. There's nothen to be afeerd of.'

'Ye'll find the grass a soft bed,' exclaimed
the carpenter.

'Thank you,' I answered; 'but since I am
detained here against my will, allow me at
least to choose my own mattress. Should you

want me, you'll find me about eighty paces yonder, where there's some clean sand betwixt the bushes.' I pointed to a spot a little distance past the curve of the lagoon.

'It don't signify to us where ye sleep, sir,' exclaimed Lush ; ' we shan't be wanting ye till the morning, by which time I hope you'll have recollected the distance Capt'n Braine named. If you should feel a-dry in the night ye'll find a kettle-full of rum-and-water alongside yon breaker that's standing upright.'

'Thanks,' said I ; 'good-night.'

There was a rumbling sleepy answer of ' good-night' from amongst them.

The spot I had chosen gave me a clear view of the lagoon, and by consequence of the boat. There was no grass here, and the bushes were small and stunted, as though starved by the sandy character of the soil. Yet they furnished a dark surface, amid which I could crawl on my hands and knees without risk of being seen from the place occupied by the men. I sat down to wait and watch. Over the tops of the bushes alongside of me I could just distinguish the figures of the sailors when one or another of them rose apparently to obtain a drink from the kettle.

After I had been seated some twenty minutes
or so, I spied one of them walking towards
the boat. His dark shape showed with tolerable distinctness when he emerged from the
comparative obscurity of the herbage into the
dull gleam of the stretch of coral foreshore.
He entered the boat, and then I lost sight of
him, for the water past him lay in a trembling
sheet of gloom, and his outline was absorbed
in it. From time to time I could hear the
voices of the seamen conversing ; but shortly
after eleven all was silent amongst them, and
then the indescribable hush of the great ocean
night settled down upon the lonely rock.

There was nothing in the stirring of the
bushes to the wind, in the dim and delicate
seething in the lagoon, in the hollower note
of surf lightly tumbling at the back of the
island, to vex this vast oppressive stillness.
I thanked God that there was no moon ; yet
could have earnestly prayed for more wind
and for a few clouds to obscure something
of the small fine spangling of the atmosphere
by the stars. I could see no light upon the
barque ; she lay in a little heap of faintness,
what with her white sides and hanging white
topsails, out in the gloom.

Presently, when I had supposed that all hands saving the fellow in the boat were sleeping, I saw a figure slowly coming my way. I gathered by his posture, as I dimly discerned it, that he was staring among the bushes as he advanced. He slightly lurched as he stepped, and it was not until he was within twenty feet of me that I perceived he was the carpenter. I pillowed my head on my arm, drew my feet up, and feigned to be in a sound slumber. He arrived abreast of me, stood looking a little, and then went slowly back to the others.

The scheme I had made up my mind to adventure was one of extraordinary peril. Yet I was quite certain that the dreadful risk would provide me with my last, indeed my only chance. I was now immovably convinced that though Captain Braine's story of the existence of the island was a fact, his assurance of a large fortune in hidden gold was a madman's fancy. The men would be finding this out; what they would then do, I could not conjecture; but the menace involved in their lawlessness, their rage of disappointment, their determination (certain to follow) to find their account in the barque and her

cargo at all costs, was so heavy, so fraught
with deadly peril to Miss Temple and myself,
that I was resolved that night to make one
prodigious dash for liberty, leaving the rest
to fate.   Once during that day it had occurred
to me to make a rush for the boat and shove
off, leaving the men without any means of
pursuing me ; but a little consideration showed
me that the risks of such an attempt were all
too fearfully against me.   If I valued my life
for my own as well as for the girl's sake, I must
not fail ; and yet failure seemed almost certain.
Before I could have liberated the line that
secured the boat, sprung into her, lifted one
of her heavy oars to shove her off with, the
men, who had always been working within a
hundred and fifty yards of the beach, would
have been upon me.   Or supposing I had
• managed to slide the boat a few fathoms away
before they arrived, half of them would have
been probably able to swim faster than I could
scull the clumsy fabric, whilst my erect figure
must have supplied an easy mark for the
stones which those remaining on shore would
have hurled at me.   No ! I had mused upon
and then utterly dismissed that scheme, coming

back to my first resolution, which I now lay waiting for the right moment to execute.

At half-past twelve by my watch, which the starlight enabled me to read, the man who had first entered the boat came out of it, and was replaced by another, whose figure I followed with my sight as he passed across the beach and disappeared in the little structure. For another hour I continued to watch, to wait, to hearken with every sense in me strained to its acutest limit; during which time the island continued sunk in the profoundest stillness of this midnight, saving always the noise of the rippling of waters and of the breezy stirring of the bushes. Then with a few words of appeal to God for courage and support, I started to crawl round past the spot where the men were sleeping, that I might arrive at the beach under cover of the tall grass, which would hinder them from observing my form as I approached the tree to which the boat's line was secured.

The soil ran in a sandy trail through the bushes hereabouts, and I got along pretty nimbly, crawling noiselessly, feeling ready to burst at times, owing to the almost unconscious holding of my breath, forced upon me by my apprehension lest I should be observed or overheard. Presently, coming to the trees at whose base the men had dug, I stood up, not fearing detection here, and very rapidly gained the growth of bushes which darkened a space of land to the north, betwixt the place where the men lay and the broad shelf of white beach where, as the fellows had supposed, the Spanish brigantine had driven ashore. I now dropped on my knees and hands again, and in this posture skirted the high herbage that grew down to where the coral grit provided no soil for such vegetation, until I came to the tree, close up against which I rose, that my shape might appear as a part of the trunk. Then, with an eager, trembling hand, I cast the line adrift, and sinking again on my knees and hands, crawled upon the dark surface of the verdure to where it went nearest to the northern horn of the lagoon, where, still crouching, I remained for a little space watching.

In a few minutes the liberated boat, feeling the action of the wind, slowly floated off.

At every instant I was prepared to hear a shout from the shore or from the fellow who was supposed to be at watch in the boat.

Yet it soon grew plain that my utmost hopes were to be confirmed by the heavy rum-influenced slumber that had overtaken the watchman, and that lay in lead upon the closed lids of the wearied sailors upon the grass. My heart was loud in my ears as I crouched watching. Presently the boat had slipped to some considerable distance from the shore, and was sliding seawards out to the wide yawn of the lagoon broadside to the ripples and the breeze. Then, pulling off my coat and waistcoat, and shoes and small-clothes, I crawled down on to the clear gleam of the beach, waded into the water, and struck out for the barque.

I was a fairly good swimmer; of old the exercise had been one of delight to me. The water was cool, but not chilling; I seemed to find a buoyancy in me, too, as from excess of brine in the dark surface, through which I gently pushed at first, lest I should raise a light of phosphorescence about me. At intervals I would pause, faintly moving my arms that I might keep myself afloat, and hearkening in a very agony of expectation. But all continued silent ashore. Now and again I caught sight of the boat as she went drifting seawards; but the shadow of the night lay thick upon the breast of the sea, and the small structure was sunk in it in a blending that eluded the gaze.

When I considered I had swum far enough to render any such sea-glow as my movements would kindle about me invisible from the island, I put my whole strength into my arms and legs and swam with a vigour that speedily began to tell. The dim heap of faintness which the barque had made grew definable with the stealing out of its proportions. The outline of the hull shaped itself; then I could see the clear line of the yards and spars ruling the starry sky with the vaporous-like folds of the topsails hanging. I felt no fatigue, no cold; the silence on the land filled me with a spirit of exultation, and the animation of that emotion acted upon me like a cordial of enduring virtue. Gradually and surely I neared the barque; the swim was but a short one in reality, and I needed no rest, though rest I could easily have obtained by floating on my back for a while. Within twenty minutes from my first cautious taking of the water, my hand was upon the lowest rung of the rope gangway ladder that lay over the side.

I held by it a little, to take breath and to listen. I had seen no figures on the vessel as I approached : but I knew that Forrest was on board, that the very piratical cast of the rogue's character would render him alert and perceptive ; that the moment he spied me he would guess a stratagem, and be upon me ; and that it was my business to be before him, or to be prepared for his first spring, armed, as I knew him to be, with the sailor's invariable weapon, the sheath-knife.

CHAPTER XLI

WE SAIL AWAY

It did not take me long to recover my breath. The swim had, indeed, comparatively speaking, been a short one ; there was no tide that I had been in any degree sensible of ; and I had lost nothing but breath, thanks to my eagerness, to the riotous tumult of spirits that had nerved my limbs with steel and rendered me unconscious of fatigue. I crawled up the ladder and peered over the rail. The gloom lay heavy upon the quarter-deck and waist, and objects were hard to distinguish. All was motionless, however, there and on the forecastle ; but I could now discern two figures walking on the poop on the port side. The spanker-boom and mizzen-mast and the several fittings of skylight and companion, and so on, had concealed them from my observation whilst I swam, approaching the ship as I had on the starboard side. Their shapes showed tolerably clear against the stars that sparkled over the rail and betwixt the squares of the rigging, and I stood staring with no more of me showing over the line of bulwarks than my head till they had come to the rail that protected the break of the poop, and I then made out that one of them was Miss Temple.

This convinced me that the other must be Wetherly, for it was not to be imagined that the girl would seek refuge from even a more frightful loneliness than hers was in the society of young Forrest.

At that instant I heard a long wild halloa dimly coming through the steady breeze from the shore. The cry was followed by another and yet another, and then it seemed to me that it was re-echoed from off the water some distance ahead of us. I sprang in a bound on to the deck, and in a breath had armed myself with an iron belaying-pin ; and now if that man were Forrest with whom Miss Temple was, I was ready for him ! In a moment I had gained the poop. The cries ashore had brought the pair to a dead halt, and they stood listening. Now that I was on the poop I perceived by the build of the figure of the

man that it was Wetherly, and rushed up to
him. The girl recoiled with a loud shriek on
seeing me, as well she might; for, having
partially undressed myself, I was clothed from
top to toe in white; I was dripping wet besides, which moulded my attire to my figure
and limbs as though I had been cast in plaster
of Paris, and my sudden apparition was as if
I had shaped myself out of the air.

'Is that you, Wetherly?' I cried.

'Great God, mum, it's Mr. Dugdale!' he
roared.

The girl uttered another shriek, came in a
bound to me and flung her arms round my
neck.

Now the halloaing ashore was incessant,
and the wild cries sounding through the wind
were as though the island had been suddenly
invaded by an army of frenzied cannibals.

'My dearest!' I cried, letting forth my
heart in that moment of being clasped and
clung to by her whom I had long loved and
was risking my life to save, 'it is I indeed!
But release me now, my darling girl. We
must get the barque under weigh instantly.
Wetherly, where is Forrest?'

'Dead, sir.'

'*Dead!*' I cried.

'Shot dead by Miss Temple's hand, sir,' he exclaimed.

The girl let fall her arms from my neck, essayed to speak, struggled a little with her breath, and fell against me in a dead swoon.

'Your coat, Wetherly,' I shouted; 'off with it, man, and make a pillow for the lady's head. Quick! If the long-boat sculls ashore and the crew enter her before we can slip, we are both of us dead men.'

He instantly pulled off his jacket; and tenderly, but swiftly, I laid the girl down, first freeing the collar of her dress and no more, for there was time for no more.

'Jump for the cabin lamp, Wetherly,' I cried; 'don't stop to ask any questions. We must knock out a shackle, and let the chain go overboard. That is what is now to be done.'

He rushed off the poop, I in his wake. The lamp was dimly burning, but it enabled us to find what we wanted in the carpenter's chest: and whilst I held the light to a shackle that was just forward of the windlass barrel, he let drive, and the cable went with a roar through the iron hawse-pipe.

'We must now get the topsail on her and blow away,' I cried.

The conviction that the men would view him as my confederate and have his life if they got aboard, put an incredible activity into his limbs, which were habitually slow of motion. My having swum to the ship made his sailorly mind comprehend without a syllable of explanation from me how I had contrived the matter. We fled to where the topsail clewlines were belayed, and let them go, and then hand over hand dragged home the sheets, which, being of chain, travelled through the sheave-holes very readily. This done, I sped as fast as my feet would carry me to the poop, and finding the helm amidships, waited to see how the wind sat with regard to the position of the ship, meanwhile bawling at the top of my lungs to Wetherly to let go the maintopsail clewlines and bring the clews home as far as his strength would enable him.

The light breeze was off the starboard quarter. I at once starboarded the helm, and, to my infinite delight, found the barque responsive to the turn of the spokes, proving that, snail-like as might be her progress, she at least had steerage way upon her. This brought the land upon the starboard beam. I then steadied the helm, quite sure that the craft would steer herself for a few minutes.

As I ran forward I witnessed Miss Temple in the act of sitting upright. I sprang to her side and lifted her to her feet, and held her for perhaps a minute with her face upon my shoulder until she should have recovered herself.

'Sit on this skylight,' I exclaimed, 'until you feel equal to assisting us, and then come to our help, for we greatly need you.'

She understood me, but was too weak and dazed as yet to be of use. The shouts from the shore were incessant. The men had heard the chain cable as it rattled through the hawse-pipe, and I judged they were yelling to the ship, as though hailing Forrest; but they were too far distant for their syllables to reach us. I spent a breathless moment in sweeping the sea towards the mouth of the lagoon, and on a sudden saw the boat like a drop of ink on the star-touched shadow of the water; but I heard no sounds of her being sculled—which would be the fellow's only

chance of getting ashore—nor could I catch
the least sign of his figure.

My immediate business now was to get
the foretopsail mast-headed as best we could.
There was a little winch just abaft the mainmast. Shouting out my intentions to Wetherly,
I bent on the first length of rope I met with
to the hauling part of the topsail halliards and
brought it to the winch, where I took some
turns with it. As I did this, Miss Temple descended the poop ladder.

'Have you strength to hold on to this
rope?' I cried to her.

'Oh, yes,' she answered.

I put it into her hand, bidding her do no
more than keep a light strain upon it, that it
might not slip; and in a moment the little
winch was rattling with the chirruping of its
pawls going straight up in the air like an end-
less cocking of muskets to Wetherly's and my
vigorous arms.

By this means we contrived to hoist the
foretopsail, though not, as will be supposed,
to a 'taut leech,' as sailors call it. Yet the
cloths showed a wide surface to the wind, and
already the nimble frame of the little barque,
yielding to the summer pressure aloft, was

sliding along very nearly as fast as the men could have urged the heavy long-boat through the water, supposing them to have recovered her and to be in pursuit. Whilst Wetherly manœuvred with the maintopsail halliards in readiness for hoisting the yard, I once again hurried aft to the wheel, to make sure of the course of the barque. She was drifting dead before the small breeze with her head at about east-by-north, and already had brought the island veering upon the quarter, lying down there in a lump of blackness in the starlit gloom, with just the gleam of the bit of northern coral sea-board glancing off the dusk of the shelving reef. From time to time I could hear the fellows shouting, but their voices were now sounding thin, weak, and remote. The star-flakes in the black water astern trembled to the mild passage of the wind; and sparks of the sea-fire, like golden seed, churned up in our wake mingled with those delicate crystal reflections. With an eager passionate prayer upon my lip that this steady draught would hold, I regained the main-deck; and all being ready, Wetherly and I revolved the winch, Miss Temple holding on as before, and the yards slowly mounted till we could 'heave and pawl' no further.

'Now, Wetherly,' I shouted, 'jump aloft and loose that foresail. Pass your knife through the gaskets. Don't wait to cast them adrift.'

Then catching up the girl's hand, which I pressed to my lips before speaking, I asked her to accompany me to the wheel, that she might hold the helm steady and keep the barque straight before the wind.

'There is no time,' I exclaimed as I hastened aft with her, 'to utter more than the few syllables necessary to effect our escape. We must heap all the canvas we can manage to spread upon the ship. We must contrive to blow away out of sight of that island before the breeze fails, or the men will be giving chase in the long-boat.'

She grasped the spokes in silence. The binnacle lamp was unlighted, and the card lay in gloom. I bade her take note of a star that stood like a jewel at the extreme end of the starboard main-yardarm, and swiftly directed her how to move the wheel, if that star swung from the end of the spar, so as to bring it back again to its place. I then sprang to the

main-rigging, and climbed with the activity of
one to whom the loss of a minute may mean
life or death, to the height of the topgallant
yard, the sail of which I loosed, and then
came hand over hand down to the deck by
the stay. The barque was but a toy of a ship
at the best, and after the pyramidal heights
reared by the Indiaman, her tops and cross-
trees looked but a leap from the deck. I
had sheeted home the topgallant-sail before
Wetherly had let fall the foresail. I sum-
moned him to the halliards, and when the
sail was set, we let go the fore clew garnets
and hauled the sheet aft. Then we hoisted
the foretopmast staysail and other light fore
and aft sails ; and in order to get as much
weight out of the wind as there blew in it, we
braced the yards somewhat forward, that the
fore and aft canvas might draw. When this
was done, I raced aft to the wheel and put it
down.

No sooner did the little barque feel the air
off her beam than she gently sloped her spars
to it with a small spitting of froth at her cutwater, and in a few minutes she was gliding
along like a yacht, reeling off a fair six knots
with water smooth as ice to travel over, small

as was the amount of canvas we had made shift to spread. But I could do no more. My strength had failed me, and I was incapable of further exertions. It was not the fatigue of the swim merely, nor my red-hot haste and maddened labours since I had boarded the barque; the frightful hours of expectation, of anticipation, of hopes and fears, and of waiting, that I had passed upon the accursed island since sundown were now heavily telling upon me.

'Hold the wheel, will you, Wetherly,' said I. 'I am pretty nearly spent. I must rest a bit. Thanks be to God, we are safe now, I believe;' and so saying, I sunk wearily upon the stern gratings.

Miss Temple went hastily to the cabin, carrying with her the lamp with which Wetherly had kindled the mesh in the binnacle. In a few minutes she returned with a tumbler of brandy-and-water, which she put to my lips. I swallowed the contents greedily, for I was not only parched with thirst, but my nerves sorely needed the stimulant. I took her hand and brought her to sit by my side, and continued to caress her hand, scarcely equal for more just then than a few rapturous

exclamations over our deliverance, the delight
I felt in being with her again, the joy in believing that I should now be able to redeem
my promise and restore her in safety to her
mother. Her replies were mere murmurs.
Indeed, her own emotions were overwhelming.
I could hear her sobbing; then see her by
the starlight smiling; but she kept her eyes
fixed on my face; soaked as I still was to the
skin with salt water, she leaned against me, as
though she needed the assurance of actual
contact to convince her that I was with her
once more.

But by this time the island had melted
into the scintillant dusk of the sky. Nothing
showed but the liquid sweep of the indigo
line of horizon. Another hour of such sailing as this would convey us out of all possibility of reach of the long-boat, supposing
the men should recover her; for she was
without mast or sail; the utmost exertion of
the rowers could scarcely get more than three
or three and a half miles an hour out of her;
then again I had shifted the barque's course,
and would shift it again presently.

'Tell me now about Forrest?' I exclaimed,

breaking a silence of fatigue and emotion that had lasted some few minutes.

I felt the shudder that ran through my companion in the clasp of her hand.

'Did I understand that you shot him?'

'It is too dreadful to speak of,' she said in a low voice.

'It was like this, sir,' exclaimed Wetherly. 'Forrest and me had agreed to keep a four hours' lookout. He was to stand from eight to twelve. I lay down on the fo'c'sle, believing the lady safe below, where she'd been pretty nigh ever since you and the men went ashore. I was awoke by a noise that sounded to me like the report of a gun. It was then about six bells, sir. I thought I'd just walk aft to see if all was right with the lady. Audacious as I knew that there fellow Forrest to be, speaking of him as a fo'c'sle hand, and capable of any sort of hinsolence and mutiny and the likes of that, I had no fear of him whilst he was left alone to keep a lookout with the hentertainment of thinking about the money him and his mates was to dig up. Well, as I reached the quarter-deck the lady came out of the cabin. The light was burning dim, just as you found it when you came aboard. She held a pistol in her hand, and she says to me quite coolly : " A man came into my cabin just now. I heard him trying the handle of my door, and I took up this pistol, and when he walked in, I said : "Who are you ? What do you want ? " he answered ; and I pointed my pistol at him and fired. I believe I have killed him. Will you go and see ? " I thought she was walking in her sleep, so quiet she talked. I went to her cabin, and saw Forrest lying upon the deck. I turned him over, and he was stone dead ; shot through the heart, I reckon. I dragged his body into your cabin, where it's a-lying now. The lady then asked to keep company with me on the poop ; and so it was you found us a-walking together, sir.'

'Brave Louise !' I murmured, moved to the utterance of her Christian name, though this was the first time I had ever given it her, close and ceaseless as our association had been. Yet an instant's reluctance, regret, or bashfulness followed my pronunciation of it— even at such a moment as that !—to the memory that arose in me with the velocity of thought of the proud eyes, the haughty coldness of the lofty, disdainful, elegant Miss Temple of the *Countess Ida.*

But what she had done was a thing not to be referred to again now. I felt the piteousness of her distress, shame, and horror in her silence : by-and-by she would be able to speak of it collectedly, if there were need indeed to recur to it at all.

'No fear of the boat overhauling us, now, I think, Wetherly ? ' I exclaimed.

' Lord, no, sir ; without e'er a sail to spread either. That swim of yourn was a bold venture, Mr. Dugdale. Ye must ha' managed the job in first-rate style. Wasn't no lookout kept ? '

His questions led me into telling the story. Miss Temple listened eagerly, our hands remaining locked ; again and again she broke into an exclamation with some cry of alarm, some ejaculation of sympathy. 'You called me brave just now,' she said ; ' but how is your behaviour to be expressed ? '

' D'ye think there's any chance of the men recovering that boat ? ' inquired Wetherly. ' The chaps told me when they came aboard to furl the canvas that there was nothen to eat or drink upon the island saving what they'd taken. If they should lose the boat, it must go hard with them, sir.'

'They will not lose their boat unless the fellow who was in charge of her lay dead drunk in her bottom: an improbability; for I saw him walk on steady legs to her. My one chance lay in his being asleep. Make your mind easy: he was awakened long ago by the yells of the men, and by this time the boat lies snug at the beach of the lagoon. But why should you have any feeling for the brutes? They would have cut your throat had they succeeded in boarding us. What happened when you were asleep should be indication enough for you of the character of the ruffians, a pretty good warrant of the sort of treatment we might have expected at their hands later on, gold or no gold.'

'Mr. Dugdale,' he answered, 'all I can say is I'm thankful to the Lord to be where I am. I shall be desperate glad, I shall, when this here woyage is over. I should only just like to see my way to getting enough out of it to set up for myself ashore, for this here's been a job as has properly sickened me of the sea, and so I don't mind telling ye, sir.'

'There'll be the salvage of this craft,'

said I; ' you can have my share, and I'm sure
Miss Temple will give you hers.'

' Oh, certainly,' she exclaimed.

' Then there'll be your own share,' I went
on. ' We have to carry the ship in safety to
a port first of all. If we can't pick up hands
as we go along, we three will have to manage
as best we can. I don't doubt we shall contrive it; and then you will easily see your
way to a few hundreds.'

I saw him grin broadly by the mingled
light of the binnacle and star-shine. It
was proper to fill him with hope, and to
present to his limited understanding some
thing definite to work upon. There had
been nothing in his behaviour to render me
much obliged to him. He had chosen neutral
ground in this business, with a little inclination to the safer side: and though he had
ventured upon several promises, I had never
secretly regarded him as a man who would
prove heroically useful at a pinch. However, he was absolutely essential to our safety
now, and it was politic that I should seem
grateful; though, to be sure, there was always
the instinct of self-preservation to keep him
straight; by which I mean that he was as

eager to end this extraordinary ramble as I was.

He asked me several questions about the gold, and talked as if he believed that the men might yet meet with it; but my answers seemed to convince him after a little, and I saw him wagging his head whilst he exclaimed: 'It was at the foot of a clump of trees, I know; I clearly recollect the yarn as Wilkins gave it, and his memory couldn't have gone wrong, for he arrived fresh with it from the cabin. If they've dug at the roots of all the trees abreast of the beach, as you say, sir, and the money ain't there, then goodnight! It's the hallucination I always said it was; and for my part give me two pound of honest salvage afore two hundred thousand pound of lunatic dreamings.'

The breeze seemed to freshen as we drew away. The barque was now heeling prettily, throwing the water in a white curl of sea off her weather bow, and her wake ran far into the liquid gloom astern, into which I would again and again send a glance, governed yet by an agitation of spirits and an animation of alarm which my judgment pronounced ridiculous. I cannot express the caressing charac-

ter of Miss Temple's manner as she continued
seated close beside me. The astonishment,
the rapture, the wildly contending sensations
and emotions which had possessed her were
now giving way to a mood of happiness, of
triumphant hope, that put an indescribable
note of tender elation and grateful, joyous
sweetness into her words. If I had yet to
wonder whether she loved me, I might feel
sure that my return to her, that my presence,
filled her with emotions which came very near
to the passion of love.

But I was wet through ; and now that we
were safe, the vessel gliding with swiftness
through the clear shadow of the night, and
my shipmate Louise tranquil in the full realisation of our sudden and complete deliverance,
I could find leisure to feel a little chilly. So,
leaving her with a promise that I should shortly
return, and telling Wetherly to keep the
barque steady as she was going, I picked up
the cabin lamp, that was still feebly burning
upon the deck, and descended the companion
steps. I paused to look around me upon the
familiar interior in which Miss Temple and I
had passed so many hours of distress and
wretchedness with an exclamation of grati-

tude to God for his merciful preservation of
us, and then went to my cabin to habit myself in such dry garments as I might find in
Captain Braine's locker. I opened the door,
but recoiled with an involuntary cry. I had
forgotten Forrest! and there lay the dead body
of the man right in front of me. Twice, now,
had that little square of carpet been stained
by human blood. I was horribly shocked by
the spectacle of the corpse ; but it was necessary that I should change my clothes, and I
had to undergo the torture of being watched
by those half-closed ghastly eyes, to which
twenty expressions of life were imparted by
the stirring of the dim flame in the lantern
whilst I sought for and attired myself in dry
apparel. This done, I made a brighter flame,
and then held the light to the dead face, that
I might be sure the villain had no life in
him. No gibbeted body that had been swinging in chains for a month could be deader.
I entered the cuddy, hung up the lamp, and
went on deck.

'Miss Temple,' I exclaimed, 'will you
kindly hold the wheel for a few minutes?

She rose and grasped the spokes.

Wetherly understood me, and followed me below in silence.

'We must toss the body overboard,' said I; 'there can be no luck for the ship with such an object as that as a part of her freight, and Miss Temple must be helped to forget the horror of the night that's going.'

Between us we picked up the corpse, very quickly conveyed it through the companion hatch, went forward with it where the darkness lay heavy, and dropped it over the bulwarks.

'That's how they would have served you, sir,' said Wetherly.

'And you,' said I.

'Yes, my God, I know it!' he answered in a voice of agitation.

We returned to the wheel, which Wetherly took from Miss Temple, who seated herself with me just behind it on the gratings, and there we held a council. Our business must be to get to a port as soon as possible. Should we head away for the Islands of the Low Archipelago, bearing north-west with a chance of falling in with a vessel cruising amongst them who would lend us two or three men to help us in navigating the barque, or should we steer a due east course for Valparaiso, that lay about two thousand six hundred miles distant?

Our resolution was rapidly formed. The islands might yield us no help; there was also the risk of running ashore upon the hundred reefs of that then little known navigation; abundance of the natives of the groups were man-eaters, and we certainly had not delivered ourselves from the perils we ran through enforced association with the carpenter and his crew merely to ingloriously terminate our adventures by serving to appease the appetite of a little population of blacks.

No; it must be Valparaiso. There we should find a city with every species of convenience: a consul to advise and assist us; shops where Miss Temple could make all necessary purchases; a choice of large ships for the passage home. The ocean we were traversing was the Pacific, and the time of year in it summer; there was nothing greatly to alarm us then in the contemplation of the possibility of our having to work the barque to the South American coast without more help than the three of us could provide. It would be necessary to keep the vessel under

easy canvas, that we might always be equal
to the occasion of a sudden change of weather,
and that, to be sure, would protract the run.
But a few weeks more or less of old ocean
would be as nothing to us now that we were
masters of our lives and liberty, now that we
should know every day was bringing us
something nearer to our distant home, that
all the horrors with which our future had
but a few hours before been crowded were
gone.   As we conversed, talking with exultation of our escape, arranging for keeping
watches, planning about the cooking of the
food, and concerting twenty other measures
of a like sort, the day broke; the stars died
out in the east; the pale green of dawn went
lifting like a delicate smoke into the shadow
of the zenith; the light broadened fast, and
the sun soared into a flashing day of cloudless
heaven and of dark-blue ocean wrinkled by
the breeze.   With a telescope in my hand I
sprang on to the grating and slowly circled
the sea-line with the lenses.   The water
brimmed bare to the sky on all sides.

'We are alone,' said I, dismounting and
taking Miss Temple by the hand whilst I
looked fondly into her face.   'When we were

on the wreck, it was our misery to hunt the
ocean with our gaze and find ourselves alone;
and now, though we are still at sea, loneliness is delightful—for it is escape, freedom,
the promise of home.'

Her eyes filled with tears.

CHAPTER XLII

CONCLUSION

I HAVE kept you long at sea. With my escape in the barque from Captain Braine's island in company with my shipmate Louise, the story of my adventure—the narrative, indeed, of the romance of the wreck—virtually ends. Yet you will wish to see Miss Temple safely home; you will desire to know whether I married her or not; you will also want to hear the latest news of the people of the *Countess Ida*, to learn the fate of the Honourable Mr. Colledge, of the crew of the *Magicienne's* cutter, and of the carpenter Lush and his merry gold-hunting men. All may be told in the brief limits of a chapter.

For five days Wetherly and Miss Temple and myself navigated the barque without assistance. We managed it thus: the girl took her turn in steering the vessel, and after a very few trials steered with the expertness of a trained hand. I can see her now as she stands at the wheel: her fine figure clear cut against the soft Pacific blue over the stern; her dark and shining eyes bent upon the compass card, or lifting in the beauty of the shadow of their lashes to the white canvas; her hands of ivory delicacy grasping the spokes, and always a smile of sweetness and gladness and hope for me when our glances met. To think of the haughty, aristocratic Miss Louise Temple reduced to it! But she did a deal more than that: she helped us to pull and haul; she cooked for us, she kept a lookout, walking the weather-deck whilst Wetherly steered and I was resting. No complaint ever left her lips; she was gentle and happy in all she did. The sea had dealt with her to some purpose; and she was now as sweet, tender, compliant, as she was before self-willed, insolent, and objectionable in all things but her beauty.

The struggle, indeed, would have been a desperate one for us but for the weather. The small but steady sailing breeze that had blown us away from the island continued with a shift of three points only in those five days, and a trifling increase one night, so that we had never occasion to start a sheet or let go a halliard; nothing more were we called upon to do with the gear than to slacken away the braces.

It was on the afternoon of the fifth day that we fell in with a Peruvian man-of-war brig. She backed her topsail and sent a boat. The young officer in command spoke French very fluently, and Miss Temple and I between us were able to make him understand our story. He returned to his ship to report what I had said, and presently came back with a couple of Irish seamen, to whose services to help us to carry the barque to Valparaiso we were, he said, very welcome. This I considered an extraordinary stroke of fortune, for in so slender a ship's company as we should still make it was of the utmost consequence that all orders given should be perfectly and instantly intelligible. The Peruvian brig was bound on a cruise amongst the islands, and I earnestly entreated the officer to request his commander to head first of all for the reef upon which I had left Lush and his men, that they might be taken off, if they had not recovered their boat.

Down to this point, the three of us in one

fashion and another had managed so fairly
well, that the acquisition of the two Irish
seamen communicated to me a sense of being
in command of a very tolerable ship's company. Miss Temple and I could now enjoy
some little leisure apart from a routine that
had been harassing with its vexations and
incessant demands upon our vigilance. Night
after night descended upon us in beauty; the
warm wind blew moist with dew; the reflection of the rich and trembling stars quivered
in cones of an icy gleam amid the ripples of
the breeze-brushed sea; the curl of new moon
shone in the west in the wake of the glowing
sun to rise nightly fuller and more brilliant
yet, till for awhile the barque sailed through
an atmosphere that was brimful of the greenish
glory of the unclouded planet. There was
scarcely, indeed, a condition of this tender
tropic passage to Valparaiso that was not
favourable to sentiment. Yet my pride rendered it an obligation upon me that before I
spoke my love I must make sure of the girl's
own feelings towards me. I watched her with
an impassioned eye; I listened to every word
that fell from her lips with an ear eager to
penetrate to the spirit of her meaning; a

smile that seemed in the least degree am-
biguous would keep me musing for a whole
watch together. Then I would inquire
whether I could in honour ask her to be my
wife until my protection and care for her had
ceased, and she stood to me in the position
she had occupied when we had first met
aboard the Indiaman. But to this very fine
question of conscience I would respond with
the consideration that if I did not ask her
now, I must continue in a distracting state of
suspense and anxiety for many weeks, running, indeed, into months—that is to say,
until we should reach home; that she might
misconstrue my reserve, and attribute it to
indifference; that to make her understand
why I did not speak would involve the
declaration that my honour was supposed to
regard as objectionable.

But all this self-parleying simply signified
that I was waiting to make sure of her answer
before addressing her. In one quarter of an
hour one fine night, with a high moon riding
over the topsail yardarm and the breeze
bringing an elfin-like sound of delicate singing
out of the rigging, it was settled! A glance
from her, a moment of speaking silence,

brought my love to my lips, and standing with her hand in mine in the shadow of a wing of sail curving past the main-rigging, with the brook-like voice of running waters rising, I asked her to be my wife.

There was hesitation without reluctance, a manner of mingled doubt and delight. I had won her heart; and her hand must follow; but her mother, her dearest mother! Her consent must be obtained; and from what she said in disjointed sentences, with earnest anxiety to say nothing that might give me pain, with a voice that trembled with the emotions of gratitude and affection, I gathered that Lady Temple's matrimonial schemes for her daughter soared very considerably above the degree of a commoner.

'But, Louise, I have your love?'

'Yes, yes, yes! my love, my gratitude, and my admiration.'

'And you need but your mother's consent to marry me?'

'Yes, and she will consent. This long association—this astonishing adventure '——

'Ay, but there is no obligation of marriage in *that*. I have your love, and your mother will consent because you love me?'

She fixed her eyes on my face, and by the haze of moonlight floating off the sand-white planks into the shadow in which we stood, I saw such meaning in them that the sole sequel of my interpretation of it must be to put my lips to hers.

'My first kiss, Louise! My God! how little did I dream of this happiness when I used to look at you and almost hate you aboard the *Countess Ida!*'

But enough of this. It all happened so many years ago now, that I am astonished by my memory that enables me to put down even so much of this little passage of my experiences with Louise as I have written.

After days of delightful weather and prosperous winds, we came to an anchor at Valparaiso. I at once waited upon the British consul, related my story, delivered over the ship, and was treated by him with the utmost courtesy, consideration, and hospitality. A large English vessel was sailing for Liverpool eight days after the date of our arrival. I inspected her, and promptly took berths for myself and Miss Temple; and the rest of the time we spent in providing ourselves with the necessary outfit for another long voyage.

The consul informed me that the deposition I made as to the *Lady Blanche* would suffice in respect of the legal manœuvring that would have to follow, and that I was at liberty to sail whenever I chose. I empowered him to hand over any salvage money that might come to me to Wetherly, whom I also requested to call upon me when he should arrive in England, that I might suitably reward him for the very honest discharge of his duties from the time of our leaving the island in the barque.

I will not pretend that our passage home was uneventful. Out of it might readily be spun another considerable narrative; but here I may but glance at it. The ship was named the *Greyhound*. She was a tall, black, soft-wood-built ship, of American birth, with a white figurehead, and fine lines of planking, and three lofty skysail poles, and an almost perpendicular bow, and she had, to use the old term, the sailing qualities of a witch. There went with her a number of passengers, Spanish and English, who, thanks, I suppose, to the gossip of the British consul and his wife and family, were perfectly informed of every article of our story, and in consequence made a very great deal of us—of Miss Temple in particular. But how great had been the change wrought in her character! No more supercilious airs, haughty looks, chilling glances of contemptuous surprise. Her sweetness and cordiality rendered her as completely a favourite as she had been before disliked and feared by her fellow-passengers of the Indiaman.

It took her a long while, however, to recur without exquisite distress to the man Forrest whom she had shot. But I was never weary of putting the matter before her in its just light; and at last she suffered me to persuade her that what she had done it had been her duty to do, that every law of God and man was at the back of such a deed to justify and even consecrate it, and that so far from suffering the recollection to render her wretched, she should proudly honour herself for the instant's coolness, courage, and presence of mind she had exhibited at sight of the scoundrel. Yet it was inevitably a memory to linger darkly with her for some time.

Our being incessantly together from the hour of our sailing down to the hour of our arrival strengthened her love for me, and her

passion became a pure and unaffected sentiment. This I could have by no means sworn
it was when I spoke my love to her in the
Pacific. I was sure that she liked me, that
she even had a warm affection for me, inspired
by gratitude and by esteem for as much of my
character as she could understand in my
behaviour to her. But I could not satisfy
myself that she loved me, or that, subject to
her mother's approval, she would have consented to marry me, but for our extraordinary
experiences, that had coupled us together in
an intimacy which most people might consider
matrimony must confirm for her sake if not
for mine.

But if that had ever been her mood—she
never would own it—it ripened during this
voyage into a love that the most wretchedly
sensitive heart could not have mistaken. And
now it remained to be seen what reception
Lady Temple would accord me. She would
be all gratitude, of course; she would be
transported with the sight and safety of her
daughter; but ambition might presently do-
minate all effusion of thankfulness, and she
would quite fail to see any particular obligation on her daughter's part to marry merely

because we had been shipmates together in a series of incredible adventures.

But all conjecture was abruptly ended on our arrival by the news of Lady Temple's death. A stroke of paralysis had carried her off. The attack was charged to her fretting for her daughter, of whose abandonment upon the wreck she had received the news from no less a person than the Honourable Mr. Colledge. Let me briefly describe how this had come about.

When the cutter containing Mr. Colledge and the men of the *Magicienne* had lost sight of the wreck in the sudden vapour that had boiled down over it, the fellows, having lost their lieutenant and being without a head, hurriedly agreed to pull dead away before the wind in the direction of the Indiaman, not doubting that she would be lying hove-to, and that they must strike her situation near enough to disclose the huge loom of her amidst the fog. They missed her, and then, not knowing what else to do, they lashed their oars into a bundle and rode to it. It was hard upon sunset when a great shadow came surging up out of the fog close aboard of them. It was the corvette under reefed topsails. The cutter

was within an ace of being run down. Her
crew roared at the top of their pipes, and
they were heard; but a few moments later
the *Magicienne* had melted out again upon
the flying thickness. The boat, however, had
been seen, and her bearings accurately taken;
and twenty minutes later, the corvette again
came surging to the spot where the cutter
lay. Scores of eyes gazed over the ship-of-
war's head and bulwarks in a thirsty, piercing
lookout. The end of a line was flung, the
boat dragged alongside, and in a few minutes
all were safe on board. Colledge related the
story of the adventure to his cousin—how the
lieutenant had fallen overboard and was
drowned, as he believed; how Miss Temple
and I were left upon the wreck, and were yet
there. But the blackness of a densely foggy
night was now upon the sea; it was also blowing hard, and nothing could be done till the
weather cleared and the day broke.

That nothing was done, you know. When
the horizon was penetrable, keen eyes were
despatched to the mastheads; but whether it
was that the light wreck had drifted to a
degree entirely out of the calculations of Sir
Edward Panton, or that his own drift during

the long, black, blowing hours misled him, no
sign of us rewarded his search.   For two days
he gallantly stuck to those waters, then aban-
doned the hunt as a hopeless one, and proceeded on his voyage to England.

Mr. Colledge on his arrival immediately
thought it his duty to write what he could
tell of the fate of Miss Temple to Lady
Temple's brother, General Ashmole.   The
General was a little in a hurry to communicate
with poor Lady Temple.   His activity as a
bearer of ill tidings might perhaps have found
additional animation in the knowledge that if
Miss Temple were dead, then the next of her
kinsfolk to whom her ladyship must leave the
bulk of her property would be the General
and his four charming daughters.   Be this as
it will, the news proved fatal to Lady Temple.
The uncertainty of her daughter's fate, doubt
of the possibility of her having been rescued
from the wreck, fears of her having met with
a slow, miserable, most dreadful death, preyed
upon such poor remains of health as paralysis
and a long term of motionless confinement had
left her ; and her maid one morning on entering her room found her dead in her bed.

The shock was a terrible one to Louise.

Again and again she had said to me that if the news of her having been lost out of the Indiaman reached her mother before she arrived home, it would kill her. And now she found her prediction verified! I was a deal grieved for the girl's sake; but it was not a thing for me to take very seriously to heart. Indeed it was not long before I got to hear that her ladyship had been an exceedingly ambitious woman, with the highest possible notions of her own importance, and of an insufferable condescension of manner; and I was assured had she lived, I should have found her a formidable, perhaps an immovable obstacle to my marriage. But had she been the most amiable of women, the stroke of her death must have been considerably softened to my mind by understanding that it made Louise the absolute mistress of a mansion and large grounds and a clear income of three thousand five hundred a year. This was very well, and quite worth being shipwrecked and kidnapped for.

But if her ladyship's death cleared the road for me in one way, it temporarily blocked it for me in another by enforcing delay. Louise must not now marry for a year. No; anything

less than a year was out of the question. It
would be an insult to the memory of an adored
parent even to think of happiness under a
twelvemonth. I resigned myself in silence to
the affliction of waiting, leaving it to time to
unsettle her resolution. She had many relatives, and she went from house to house ; but
I was never very far off. I loved her too
fondly to lose her. I had won her, and I
meant to have and hold the supreme title to
her that had come to me from old ocean.
Not that I had a doubt of her own devotion ;
I was afraid of her relatives. Some of them
were titled people ; they were all of them
social star-gazers, with their intellectual eyes
rooted upon objects that shone more splendidly
than they and higher in life's atmosphere ; and
there was such an army of them in one shape
or another, such battalions of uncles and aunts,
of cousins and connections spreading out like
the tendrils of creepers, that I feared their
influence if I did not take care to keep hovering close by to guard my Louise's heart against
any relaxation of sentiment.

Indeed, I was uneasy till I got her down
to my mother's house, and I could fill a volume
in describing the manœuvring I was forced

into to accomplish so simple a matter against the devices and stratagems of her superior connections. Already there was one young man dying of love for her. He was the eldest son of a baronet, and his mother was one of the most intriguing old wretches that ever perplexed the wishes or confounded the respectable pleasures of her fellow-creatures. Single-handed I had to fight the battle of my love against this young man, who was dying of passion, and my lady his mother, both of them backed by a large proportion of Louise's relatives; and I say I scarcely enjoyed an hour's tranquillity of mind until I had her under my mother's roof.

By this time her grief had abated; the recollection of her past sufferings lay lightly upon her mind. We were now once more together, as we had been when at sea. She soon learned to love my gentle old mother, and was so happy that after awhile her relatives ceased in despair to attempt to coax her back to them. By that time little more than six months had elapsed since our return, and, consequently, since she had received the news of her mother's death. But our being together in constant close association from morning till night, almost as much alone as ever we had been when on the wreck, what with delightful drives, delicious hand-in-hand rambles, ended in rendering me mighty impatient, and impatience is usually importunate. I grew pressing, and one day she consented to our being married at the expiration of a fortnight.

It was much too plain a wedding for such a heroine as our adventures had made Louise, but it was her own choosing. A few intimate friends of my own family, two poor but exceedingly ladylike and well-bred cousins of her own, the vicar who joined our hands, and his homely agreeable wife—these formed the company. I sent an invitation to Mr. Colledge, against the inclination of Louise, who associated him with all our misfortunes, though for my part I could have strained him to my heart on my marriage day as the involuntary promoter of all my happiness. He neither wrote nor presented himself ; but this was afterwards explained by a letter dated from Palestine, in which country he was then travelling, having made up his mind to trust himself and his fortunes as little as possible to the ocean in his determination to see the world. It was a stupid amiable letter, full of good-wishes and kindest regards, with much rambling on in reference to the wreck and his own narrow escape. I observed that he did not mention the name of Miss Fanny Crawley.

An effusion of the local good-will and sympathy was visible in the decoration of the church. Never stood any man before the altar more proud of the girl of his heart's choice than did I with Louise by my side. Beautiful she had always shown to me from the first moment of my gaze resting on her aboard the Indiaman, but never more beautiful in the eyes of my passion than on that day. The sweetness that had come to her from suffering was in every smile and look.

' We have started on another voyage now,' I whispered as we passed out of the church.

' There must be no wrecks in it,' she answered.

And for years, I thank God, it was all summer sailing with us ; but I am old now, and alone.

In those times, the round voyage to India averaged a twelvemonth, and I was unable to obtain news of the *Countess Ida* until the August that had followed the June of our

arrival at Liverpool in the *Greyhound.* I was
in London when I heard of the Indiaman as
having been reported off Deal. In the course
of a few days I despatched a note to old Keeling, addressed to the East India Docks, asking
him to come and dine with me, that I might
tell him of my adventures, and learn what
efforts he had made to recover us from the
wreck. He arrived in full shore-going fig,
with the old familiar skewered look, in the
long, tightly buttoned-up coat, and the tall
cravat and stiff collars, in which his sun-
reddened face rested like a ball in a cup.

He was heartily glad to see me, and continued to shake my hand until my arm ached
again. Of my story he had known nothing ; for
the first time he was now hearing it from my
lips. He listened with acute attention, with a
countenance over which expression chased expression ; and when I had done, seized my hand
again, and shook it long and vehemently,
whilst he complimented me on my success in
navigating the *Lady Blanche* to the island,
and on the judgment I had shown in planning
and effecting my escape from Mr. Lush and
his crew.

He had little to tell me, however, that was

very interesting. He had been blown away from the neighbourhood of the wreck; and though, when the weather cleared, he had luffed up to the spot where he believed she was to be found, he could see nothing of her. Mr. Prance was looking at the hull through his glass when the smother came driving down upon her, and saw the cutter shove off; and he believed that Miss Temple and I were in her. He had no time to make sure, for the vapour swiftly blotted the boat out of sight: But his conviction was—and Keeling owned himself influenced by it—that if they fell in with the wreck they would not find us aboard her. Poor old Mrs. Radcliffe nearly went crazy with grief and distress; and to satisfy her mind, he cruised over the supposed situation of the hull till the night fell; then satisfied that we had either perished by the capsizal of the cutter, or been picked up by the corvette, he trimmed sail for his course and proceeded.

The disaster that had befallen us, he said, had cast a heavy gloom over the ship, and it was heightened by Mrs. Radcliffe's serious illness, due to the poignant wretchedness caused her by the loss of her niece. Hemmeridge was entreated to prescribe for her, but he

sullenly refused, hoped that her illness might
be epidemical, that more might suffer than
she, and could breathe nothing but threats
of having the law of Keeling on the ship's
arrival at Bombay. However, by the time
the vessel was up with the Cape, Mrs. Radcliffe
had recovered; and when Keeling last saw
her, she seemed as hopeful as she was before
despairful of her niece being yet accounted
for.

Abreast of the Cape also, the spirits of
the passengers had sufficiently lightened to
enable some love-making to proceed briskly
amongst them.

'Much about twenty degrees of south
latitude,' said old Keeling in his dry voice,
' young Mr. Fairthorne, the fellow that lisped,
you remember, Mr. Dugdale, succeeded in
tempting that nice young lady, Constance
Hudson, to accept his hand and heart. Old
Mrs. Hudson was very well pleased, sir.
About the latitude of the Chagos Archipelago,
Mr. Emmett induced Miss Helen Trevor to
betroth herself to him. And off the Laccadive
Islands, Peter Hemskirk, to the astonishment
of all hands, deposited his person and his fortune at the feet of Miss Mary Joliffe.'

'I had thought Mr. Emmett was a married man,' I said.

'Apparently not, sir,' he answered.

'And your friend Hemmeridge?'

He replied that the surgeon consulted a solicitor at Bombay, and had no doubt been advised to take certain proceedings; but three weeks after the arrival of the ship the doctor had been thrown from a horse, and so injured in the spine and head, that he died within a fortnight.

'What he could have done I'm sure I don't know, Mr. Dugdale,' said the old fellow. 'I believe I was within my rights. Yet he might have given me trouble, and I hate law. The two fellows, Crabb and Willett, I handed over to the police. Mr. Saunders got the drug the scoundrel had used carefully analysed, and it turned out that he was right: it proved to be what he'd termed it; and I afterwards heard the stuff was not unknown in India, where it's used for some religious purposes; but in what way I don't know.'

This was all the news that old Keeling had to give me.

When I left Lush and the sailors of the *Lady Blanche* upon the reef, I had little thought of ever hearing of them again. I knew the nature of sailors. If they came off with their lives, I might be sure they would disperse and utterly vanish. Great was my surprise, then, one morning some months after my marriage, to find, on opening my morning newspaper, a column-long account of the trial of a seaman named Lush for the murder of a man named Woodward. The evidence was substantially my story with a sequel to it. The witnesses against Lush were three of the seamen of the *Lady Blanche*. The counsel for the prosecution related the adventures of the barque down to the time of my swimming off to her and sailing away with her. The boat had been in charge of the man Woodward when I detached the line to let her slip away. He had fallen into a deep sleep, overcome by fatigue and drink. The yells and roaring of the crew, one of whom had started up and observed the boat drifting out, had aroused the sleeper after the uproar had been some time continued. He was thick and stupid, went clumsily to work to scull the heavy boat ashore, and was a long time in doing it. The carpenter dragged him on to the beach and asked him if he had fallen asleep. The unfortunate wretch answered yes; the carpenter struck him fiercely; Woodward returned the blow; and, mad with rage, Lush whipped out his sheath-knife and stabbed the man to the heart.

By this time the barque had almost faded out in the gloom of the night. Pursuit was not to be thought of. They waited till daylight; but instead of putting their remaining provisions and water in the boat and heading away in search of land or a passing ship, the fools fell to digging afresh; and it was not until their little stock of water was almost gone that, being satisfied that there was no gold in that part of the shore where Captain Braine had said it lay hidden, they put to sea.

They were several days afloat before they, or at least the survivors, were rescued. Their sufferings were not to be expressed. They had been five days without water when picked up. Four of them had died, and one of the bodies had been preserved for a use that cannot be dwelt on. They were fallen in with by an English brig bound home, to the captain of which one of the sailors, who had been an old 'chum' of Woodward, told the story of the murder of that man by Lush. The skipper, not choosing to have such a ruffian as the carpenter at large in his little ship, clapped him in irons, and kept him under hatches until the arrival of the vessel in the Thames, when he was handed over to the police. I hardly wished the scoundrel hanged, richly as he deserved making such an ending; and it was with something of relief that I read when he was brought to the Old Bailey that the jury had found a verdict of manslaughter, and that he was sentenced to ten years' transportation.

To this hour I am puzzled by Captain Braine and his island. My wife uniformly believed that the gold was there, and that the poor lunatic had mistaken the bearings of the spot where it lay. My own fancy, however, always inclined to this: that from the circumstance of his having rightly described the island, which he situated on a part of the sea where no reef or land of any sort was laid down on the charts, he had actually been wrecked upon it, and suffered as he had related to me; that by long dwelling upon his terrific experience he had imported certain insane fancies into it out of his unsuspected madness when it grew upon him; until the hallucination of the gold hardened in his poor soul into a conviction. Yet I may be wrong; and, if so, then there must at this hour be upwards of a hundred and eighty thousand pounds' worth of gold coins lying concealed somewhere in the reef whose latitude and longitude you have.

THE END

PRINTED BY

SPOTTISWOODE AND CO., NEW-STREET SQUARE
LONDON

www.ingramcontent.com/pod-product-compliance
Lightning Source LLC
Chambersburg PA
CBHW030923050726
47498CB00003BA/873